DECEPTION

DECEPTION

BY

JAMES PAUL ELLISON

www.bookstandpublishing.com

Published by
Bookstand Publishing
Pasadena, CA 91101
4849_2

ISBN 978-1-953710-57-4

ACKNOWLEDGEMENTS

To Dan Gibson, a fellow author and Mayor of Natchez, MS.

To Priscilla Naughton, a true friend in Sarasota, FL.

To my brother-in-law, Jose Rodriguez Alba in Barcelona, Spain.

To Henry Diz, a lifelong friend and world traveler.

To Paul Salver, a live long friend and a CPA in Weston, Florida.

TABLE OF CONTENTS

ACKNOWLEDEMENTS v

DAY 1 – TUESDAY 1

DAY 2 – WEDNESDAY 15

DAY 3 – THURSDAY 37

DAY 4 – FRIDAY 49

DAY 5 – SATURDAY 73

DAY 6 – SUNDAY 91

DAY 7 – MONDAY 109

DAY 8 – TUESDAY 127

DAY 1 – TUESDAY

At 9:30 am on Tuesday, March 1ˢᵗ, Gavin Parker, a private investigator, age 25, exits a small insurance claim's office 20-miles outside of Gulfport, Mississippi with a new contact and possibly a new client. The lead was given to him by an insurance claim's manager, Virginia Farmer, age 66. She loves watching Gavin's surveillance videos of her own claimants.

Once back in his car, Gavin calls the phone number just given to him.

"Good morning, Morgan and Rogers Law Firm."

"This is private investigator Gavin Parker. I own Parker Investigations. Can I speak with Attorney Morgan, please? Advise him that Virginia Farmer gave me his phone number."

"Alright. I will try to locate him for you."

A minute or so later, "This is Attorney Morgan."

"Morning sir, I would like to come over and speak with you regarding investigative and surveillance assignments that I perform. I do surveillances for Virginia Farmer and she asked me to contact you."

"My 11 am client just cancelled. Can you come over at that time?"

"Sure" says Gavin. "It is 9:30 am now, no problem. See you at 11:00 am."

"Good. I will have my partner join us."

"Fantastic. I will see you both at 11:00 am."

Gavin drives 22 miles and sits in a shopping mall's parking lot. The law firm, according to his GPS is only 4 blocks away.

Gavin is known by his clients to be hard-working, honest, and on time.

At 10:55 am, Gavin is at the reception desk of Morgan and Rogers. Before entering the office, Gavin did some research on the law firm. There are 15 lawyers, and they occupy the 9th floor of the Johnson building in downtown Gulfport.

"Morning. My name is Gavin Parker. I have an appointment with Attorney Morgan."

The pretty receptionist says, "My boss told me earlier to place you in our conference room. Follow me."

Once in the empty room the receptionist asks, "Care for something to drink?"

"No thank you. What is your name, please?"

"I'm Cindy. If you need anything, I will be at my reception desk."

Gavin stands up when 2 men enter the conference room. One is carrying a file under his right arm.

"Gavin, I am Attorney Henry Morgan, and this is my partner, Attorney Tony Rogers. Please have a seat.

Once seated, Attorney Morgan says, "I have known Virginia Farmer over 30 years. She has never referred me to anyone. So, I am surprised she referred you."

"Wow, I am honored, truly honored to hear that."

"Here are our business cards. Can I have one of yours?" asks Attorney Morgan.

Gavin hands both men his business card.

Attorney Rogers, age 60, asks, "Tell us about yourself."

"Simple really. I am single and 25 years old. I was a police officer for 18 months in Meridian. I quit the force and became a private investigator. I am a one-man office. This is because it is hard to find an honest and reliable investigator. I have tried to find one. I specialize in 2 areas, surveillances, and investigations. I work hard to obtain results on all my cases."

Attorney Rodgers asks, "Why did you quit the police force?"

"The police department started requiring all uniform officers to wear body cameras. I didn't want to be judged someday by video for my actions while on patrol."

Attorney Morgan speaks next. "I called Virginia Farmer and she confirmed you are a hard worker. I have a major accident case I want to show you."

The attorney slides the file over to Gavin and says, "Take a few minutes and read the accident report."

Gavin opens the file and starts reading the narrative.

Pedestrian Dean Smith, age 24, was walking to his mailbox, located by the edge of Pass Highway, when he was struck by a semi-trailer truck. The driver of the semi, Andy Davis, age 40, claims the man suddenly stepped in front of him.

The accident occurred at 3:30 am on a Sunday morning 3 months ago. The officer on scene noted the speed limit was only 25 mph, instead of the normal 55 mph, due to highway repairs on a 12 mile stretch of Pass Highway.

Chuck Press, age 64, the owner of freight-hauling business Silver Streak, said to Sunny Eaton, the police officer on scene, "My best driver told me a young man jumped in front of his semi-truck without warning in the 900 block of Pass Highway in Gulfport. He tried to stop as quickly as he could, but that is difficult to do at 25 mph. My driver had no time to react at all. My driver did everything he could to avoid striking the man."

The police officer asked, "Where was your driver headed?"

"My driver was headed to Meridian to deliver a full load of juice when the accident occurred."

The private investigator continues to read the accident report.

The male pedestrian sustained serious injuries and was rushed to the hospital by ambulance for emergency medical care. The driver of the commercial vehicle remained on scene and was cooperating with the investigation.

The only witness, Fred Harris, age 23, said, "I drove my friend to his home. Dean said he was going to check his mailbox. I saw the semi drift over, cross the line and strike my friend."

The police officer at the accident scene, Sunny Eaton, said, "The driver attempted to slow-down and steer left, but the pedestrian was struck by the right front of the truck. The pedestrian sustained life-threating injuries because of the collision. The man survived but may be a quadriplegic.

Gavin reads where the police officer charged the semi-truck driver with careless driving and wrote next to the charge, 'Driver admits he uses his cell phone sometimes while driving'.

Gavin puts the accident report down and says to the attorneys," I can't believe the pedestrian survived after being struck by a semi at 25 mph."

Insurance Defense Attorney Morgan replies, "I know. Dean was lucky the Highway speed zone had been reduced from the normal 55 mph too. Dean's parents claim their son is a quadriplegic. According to his rehab reports, he has paralysis of both legs and his left arm. He has partial paralysis of his right arm."

"How much is Dean Smith suing your insurance client for?"

"They are seeking 20 million and may get it, too. Our driver claims the man stepped in front of him. Now who does that?"

"Wow, that much?"

"Yes. The young man is only 24. If he lives to be 80, he will need lifetime respiratory, physical therapy, and occupational therapy care. He has bowel and bladder problems, needs additional surgeries, requires 24-hour around the clock care   and must live in a specially designed house for his wheelchair. His needs just go on and on. The insurance company just purchased the young man a 50,000-dollar custom van with a power lift for his wheelchair."

The private investigator turns to the 2 lawyers and asks, "Where do I fit in all this?"

Attorney Morgan says, "I need you to place the plaintiff under surveillance. I need to see how the young man is doing and who is assisting him. I need you to interview the police officer on scene and the witness. Tell me if they will make good witnesses for court. I need you to locate and interview the plaintiff's ex-wife, see what she knows about this accident. Her name is Robin Smith. I want you to canvass the accident scene and locate any witnesses, see if any of the residences have CCTV cameras and then visit the different media outlets and get all facts they uncovered."

"What is your budget for this. I charge 100 an hour?"

"10,000 dollars to start. I will write the retainer check myself. This is the biggest case our firm has. We do not want to go to trial on this. The jury would eat us alive and give the plaintiff more than the 20 million they seek. Our goal is to settle in the 5 to 10 million range."

Gavin asks, "Why was Dean Smith walking toward his mailbox at 3:30 am on a Sunday?"

Attorney Rodgers says, "His parents were up North visiting relatives. Dean had not checked the mailbox for any mail for a few days."

Gavin replies, "That makes sense. I can investigate this claim for you both."

Attorney Morgan says, "Good to hear. Keep me updated on your progress. This way I can update my client."

"I always update my clients."

Attorney Morgan says, "That is why you have this case. My client wanted to go with one of the big private investigative firms, the ones that cover the world."

Gavin looks at his watch and says, "Let me get to work. It is 11:30 am, I will have lunch, then track down the police officer. I just can't get over the young man being struck by a loaded semi-trailer and living."

Attorney Morgan says, "Me either." The attorney writes out Gavin's retainer check and says, "Let me walk you out. I need the exercise for my legs. My secretary, Barbara, is out today. Call her if you can't reach me."

Once in his Honda, Gavin makes a telephone call to the Gulfport Police Department.

"Can I speak with Officer Sunny Eaton, please."

"The Officer is off today. He will be in tomorrow at 8 am."

"Can I leave him a message to call me?"

"Sir, I will connect you to his voice mail. One second."

"Hello. This is Officer Sunny Eaton. At the tone, leave your name, phone number and reason for calling. I will call you back within 48-hours. Have a good day."

Gavin leaves the officer a message with his cell phone number. He drives over to Subway for a footlong Ham sandwich.

Gavin uses the drive-up-window at Mercy Bank and deposits his retainer check. He calculates in his head, 'at $100 an hour that is 100 hours of investigative time'.

After his meal, Gavin drives to the crime scene and finds the rural house with the mailbox out by the highway. The private investigator starts walking down the rural highway knocking on doors. Gavin tells the occupants who he is and why he is canvassing the rural neighborhood.

Gavin says to everyone he encounters, "Afternoon. My name is Gavin Parker, I am a PI with Parker Investigations. I am trying to locate anyone that witnessed or has information about the semi-trailer striking their neighbor, Dean Smith."

There are 12 houses on that stretch of rural highway near Dean Smith's residence. All the homeowners that were home said, 'No, I was not up at 3:30 am.

Gavin would ask, "Do you go over and visit with the father or with Dean?"

Most of the occupants would say, "No. It's sad to get close and see how bad of shape the young man is in'.

A few of the people in the neighborhood would say, "I speak to the father now and then. "

One homeowner living next door to the plaintiff said, "I go over occasionally with a freshly baked apple pie. Dean loves apple pie".

Gavin walked up and down the rural highway several times trying to spot CCTV cameras. There were none. The neighborhood is about 70 years old and most homes show their age. This is a working class-type neighborhood. Of all the vehicles in the carports, only 2 were new. The people on this rural highway live paycheck-to-paycheck, that is for sure.

Gavin departs the area after speaking with the neighbors that were home, taking pictures of the crime scene, and searching for video cameras. He did not want to raise awareness to the plaintiff, that a PI was asking many questions.

Once back inside his car, Gavin calls the phone number his client gave him for Fred Harris, the star witness for the plaintiff.

"Hello?" says the female on the other end of the line.

"Afternoon. My name is Gavin Parker. I am a private investigator. I need to speak with Fred Harris."

"He went to the store to buy me some eggs. I am baking a cake. I am his mother."

"Can you please write my name and number down?

"Yes, of course. Go ahead I am ready."

Gavin gives the woman his contact information.

"Will my son know what this is about?"

"No. He is not in any trouble. I just want to know what he knows about his friend being struck by the semi-trailer."

"Very sad to hear. I still haven't contacted the family and it has been 3-months."

Gavin lies and says, "I was just with the family this morning. Dean has movement in his right arm only."

"Please tell Bill and Eva I will come-by next week."

"I sure will. Your name is?"

"Johanna Harris."

Gavin says, "I will tell Bill we spoke and that you were asking how his son is doing."

"Please do. Fred just arrived home. One minute please."

"Hello?"

Gavin introduces himself and asks Fred to meet him at the nearby Wendy's restaurant. Gavin says he is driving a grey Honda Civic 4 door.

Fred agrees and replies, "I am on my way. I drive a black-in color Ford F150."

Gavin wants to talk to Fred alone and did not want to be interrupted. Gavin was surprised the plaintiff's attorney, Joe Canton, did not warn Fred to speak to anyone, being their star witness.

Gavin arrives in the parking lot of the restaurant and waits.

About 20 minutes later, Fred pulls up next to the private investigator. Gavin motions for the witness to join him.

After Fred sits in Gavin's car, the private investigator hands the man his business card and says, "Hi Fred, I am Gavin."

Fred shakes Gavin's hand and says, "How can I help you?"

Gavin replies, "Real simple, I will be taking your statement and recording it. I will say who I am, who I represent, who my client represents, then I will ask for your basic information, ask what happened before, during and after the accident, some follow up questions and we are done."

"Alright."

"First, can I treat you to a meal?"

"Alright."

Gavin starts his car, backs up and enters the drive-up window at Wendy's. A few minutes later, both men talk as they eat their hamburgers. About 15 minutes later, both men are finished with their meals. Gavin turns his cell phone off and Fred does the same.

"Are you ready to give me your recorded statement?"

Fred says, "Sure."

"I will get started then."

Fred says, "Alright."

Before Gavin starts the recording, he says to Fred, "If I hold my hand up, it means I have a follow-up question I need answered. Once done, you can resume with your statement. An example: You say we drove. I hold up my hand and ask, who is we?"

Fred says, "I understand."

Gavin starts his tape recorder and gives the current day, date and time and says, "This is private investigator Gavin Parker. I have been retained by the law firm of Morgan and Rogers. Their client is Silver Streak Freight Forwarders. This is regarding a semi-trailer truck that struck a pedestrian, Dean Smith, that occurred near the 900 block of Pass Highway, in Gulfport, Mississippi. This accident was on Sunday, March 12th, 2020 at 3:30 am. I am speaking with Fred Harris, a witness to this incident. Please state your name for the record."

The investigator pushes his recorder closer to the gentleman.

"My name is Fred Harris."

"Mr. Harris, you are aware I am tape recording this conversation today?"

"Yes."

"I have your permission to tape record you today?"

"Yes."

"Can you tell me in your own words what you know about this incident."

"Yes. Dean and I went to a party at a friend's house on Saturday evening."

Gavin holds up his hand and asks, "What friend, the address, and time you went please?"

"Mike Miller. He lives at 437 Oak Drive in Gulfport. We went there about 11:45 pm."

"Continue please."

"At the party was Dean's wife Robin. They have been separated a few months already when Dean ran into her. Robin kept telling Dean for weeks she was filing for divorce. Dean walked over to a large crowd where Robin was seated and said, 'This is my beautiful wife, Robin'. He was so proud."

Gavin asks, "What did Robin do?"

"She stood up, reached into her purse and handed Dean her wedding ring. She then said to the crowd that was around her, "I filed for divorce yesterday morning."

Gavin raises his hand and asks, "What was Dean's reaction and was he drinking any alcohol?

"Dean had been drinking beer all night. First at his house, in my truck on the way to the party and at Mike's place. I followed Dean into the bathroom, and he was crying his eyes out. He really loved that woman. He was sobbing, 'Robin is my whole life.' He now wears her wedding ring around his neck."

Gavin holds up his hand again and says, "Dean said that?"

"Yes. Over and over the rest of the night. She was his whole life."

"Was Dean drunk?"

"I would say almost drunk. He could stand and hold a conversation."

Gavin motions for Fred to continue.

"Robin left with a guy about 1 am. We left at 2:00 am. I drove Dean home. We sat in my truck in his driveway for over an hour and drank more beer. Dean exited the truck and …"

Gavin holds up his hand and asks," What is the make, model and year of your truck."

"I drive a 2011 Ford F150 truck, black-in color."

Gavin holds up his hand one more time and asks, "How long were Dean and Robin married at that time?"

"I think 3 years."

"What happened next?"

"Dean said he was going to check his mailbox by the side of the highway. I exited my vehicle to take a quick pee by a tree'. I noticed a semi-trailer truck drift slowly across the highway and hit my friend. Dean went flying and landed in his neighbor's yard. I ran over thinking he was dead, but he was alive. I called 911 on my cell phone. I…."

Gavin holds up his hand and asks, "How long did it take for the police and ambulance to arrive?"

"They both were quick. I would say 4 minutes."

Gavin replies, "That is quick for a rural area. Continue please."

"The policeman took me to a patrol car and made me sit down. He said I was in shock."

"Gavin holds up his hand and asks, "Did you give the policeman a statement at the scene?"

"I don't know if I did or not. He called a 2nd ambulance, and I was taken to the hospital for treatment."

Gavin holds up his hand again and asks, "While at the accident scene, did you see anything else before you were taken away by ambulance?"

"I saw a fat man with long brown hair talking to the policeman. He was pointing down the highway and shouting over and over, "he suddenly stepped in front of me."

"What do you think happened between your friend and the semi-truck?

"To me, the semi drifted over and struck my friend. It was 3:30 in the morning and dark outside. Maybe the driver did not see my friend walking to his mailbox."

"What was your friend wearing the night of the accident?"

"A blue shirt, blue jeans and black shoes."

"How was the moon that night?"

"I don't think there was a moon that night."

"So dark colored clothes, no moon, means your friend was too dark for the truck driver to see till the last minute."

"I think you are right."

"How is Dean doing these days?"

"I avoid going over to see his parents. I feel guilty."

"Guilty about what?

"Dean had been drinking a lot. I should have walked him to his front door and rang the bell."

"Don't second guess yourself. That is why they call them accidents."

Fred nods his head up and down a few times.

"One more question. "Why was Dean walking toward his mailbox on a Sunday morning?"

"His parents were up North. Dean told me in the truck he hadn't checked the mailbox in days."

Gavin gives the date and time on the recording, and says, "I am ending the recording of Fred Harris at this time." Gavin turns the recorder off.

Gavin looks at his witness.

"Go see the family and find out how your friend is doing. It will make you, your friend, and his parents feel better."

"You thinks so?"

"Yes, I do. I lost a good friend years ago to cancer. Hardly any of his friends visited him in the hospital. It was sad to see. I ran into some a few weeks later and heard excuse after excuse. I know it is better. Go as soon as you can but go."

"I will."

Once alone, Gavin contacts his client's office.

"Good afternoon, Morgan and Rodgers."

"Afternoon. This is Gavin Parker. I was in your office earlier."

"Yes sir, I remember you."

"May I ask your name again, please?"

"My name is Cindy."

"Can you connect me, Cindy, with your boss, Attorney Morgan? I need to update him on my progress."

"May I call you Gavin?"

"Of course, you can. I am just a working stiff like you."

Cindy laughs and says, "Between us, my boss told me to find him, no matter what, whenever you called."

"Wow. That is cool. What are the names of the 2 owners?"

Cindy says, "Yes, it is cool. Their names are Henry Morgan and Tony Rodgers. Hold on for my bosses."

"Ok, I will."

Less than a minute later his client comes on the line, "Attorney Morgan."

"Afternoon sir, this is Gavin Parker. I wanted to give you a quick update."

"Thanks for calling. Go ahead."

"I canvased the claimant's rural neighborhood and there were no residential CCTV cameras. Most of the homes in the area are 70 years old. No neighbors were awake at 3:30 am, the time of the accident. So, no witnesses were found. A few neighbors on the rural road speaks to the father now and then. I obtained a recorded statement from the plaintiff's star witness, Fred Harris."

"Wow, you work fast. What does he have to say?"

"Mr. Fred Harris claims he did witness the semi-trailer truck drift over and strike his friend. The witness was outside peeing against a tree and saw it all. He admits the plaintiff was wearing dark clothes at the time of the accident. There was no moonlight, and this made it difficult for your client to have seen the plaintiff walking to the mailbox. Mr. Fred Harris will make a good witness in court. He appears to be honest in his statement and made eye contact with me almost the whole time."

"Wearing dark clothing and no moonlight helps our case, so that is good."

"I haven't checked the weather yet on the night of the accident. I will do so and confirm if there was a moon or not," says Gavin. "Mr. Harris went into shock and was transported by ambulance to the hospital. He does not know if he gave the police or anyone else a statement that night. Dean ran into his wife at a party the night of the accident and …"

"Did you say, a party?"

"Yes sir. He was excited to see her at his friend's party, because for months, they have been separated and she kept claiming she was going to file for divorce. He said out loud, 'Hey, it is my beautiful wife'. She stood up, handed over her wedding ring to him and said, 'not anymore, I filed for divorce yesterday'. The party was on Saturday evening and the accident was at 3:30 am Sunday."

"How did the plaintiff react to the news about his wife filing for divorce?"

"I asked the witness that and he said Dean went to the host's bathroom and cried like a baby".

"So, the plaintiff was emotional."

"Yes sir. The witness said that Dean cried a lot in the bathroom and sobbed," Robin is my whole life. The witness says Dean now wears his wife's wedding ring around his neck."

"Interesting fact. What are you going to do next on my case?"

"The witness said that the plaintiff was drinking beer all night. His last beer was in the truck just before he was struck by the semi. Tomorrow, I will speak with the police officer on scene, then the ambulance crew, then visit the different media sites to see what they know of the incident."

"I can see why Virginia wanted me to meet you. She said I would be in good hands."

"Sir, I love being a private investigator. I have your back."

"Good to hear."

"I just remembered. I asked how long it took for the police and ambulance to arrive after the semi struck the plaintiff. Fred said it was under 4 minutes."

"That was quick arrival on their part for a rural highway. Talk to you soon and thanks for the fine work so far."

James Paul Ellison

.

DAY 2 – WEDNESDAY

Gavin stays up till 3:00 am playing video games. He was sound asleep when his cell phone rang at 8:25 am.

"Hello?"

"This is Officer Sunny Eaton. Can I speak with private investigator Gavin Parker?"

"Hello Officer. I am Gavin. Your phone call woke me up."

"Sorry. What are your work hours?"

"Normally 8 am to 5 pm, but I stayed up playing video games and didn't fall asleep till around 3 am"

"I like playing chess and do the same thing. I can call you back if you want."

"Please do, if you don't mind."

"No problem. How about I call you back around 2 pm?"

"Perfect."

"What is this call all about?"

"I am a private investigator hired by the insurance defense law firm of Morgan and Rogers. This is regarding the young man that was struck by the semi-trailer truck at 3:30 am on a Sunday and lived."

"Poor chap. He survived but barely."

"I can't believe it. A semi hits him, and he is still breathing," says Gavin rubbing his eyes.

"Go back to sleep. I will call you around 2 and you can buy the coffee."

Gavin yawns and replies, "Deal."

The officer says, "Call you around 2, and hangs up.

Gavin slowly goes back to sleep.

At 2:15 pm The officer gives Gavin a call.

"This is Gavin."

"This is Officer Eaton."

 "Can we meet now? Officer."

"Perfect. How about Starbucks at 53rd Street and Copper Road?"

"Be there in 10 minutes."

"Meet you there. I am running late."

Gavin asks, "How do you take your coffee?"

"Black with a pinch of sugar. I will be wearing a black shirt."

Gavin says, "See you soon."

Gavin arrives at Starbucks and finds a quiet corner. The waiter arrives and Gavin orders 2 coffees, both with a pinch of sugar.

20 minutes later, a man walks in wearing a black shirt and Gavin stands up and walks over.

"Hello, I am Gavin. Thanks for meeting me."

"No problem, glad to help."

Gavin says, "My client represents the truck company."

"Alright. Do you know by chance how Dean Smith is doing?"

"I interviewed the neighbors on his rural highway, and they said he is in bad shape."

"How much is the family suing for?"

"The family is seeking 20-million."

"That is a lot of money," says Officer Eaton.

"It is a lot of money, but he will need a lot of care."

Officer Eaton says, "I guess we better get this statement over with. I have many errands to run."

Gavin pulls out his small tape recorder and sets it on the table.

"I will start the recording by mentioning my client, their client and I will ask your permission to tape record you. Then you will tell me about your involvement with this accident. If I hold up my hand, it means I need to clarify your answer."

Officer Eaton takes a sip of his coffee and says, "Simple enough."

Gavin speaks into his recorder.

"Today is Wednesday, June 16th, 2020. The time is 3:05 pm. This is Gavin Parker, a private investigator with Parker Investigations. I have been retained by the insurance defense law firm of Morgan and Rodgers. Their client is Silver Streak Freight Forwarders. This is regarding an accident where their driver struck Dean Smith, on Sunday, March 12th, 2020 at about 3:30 am in the 900 block of Pass Highway in Gulfport, Mississippi. This is a semi-trailer truck and pedestrian accident. In front of me is police officer Sunny Eaton. Sir, can you state your name for the record?"

"I am police officer Sunny Eaton, Gulfport Police."

"Are you aware I am tape recording your statement today?"

"Yes, I am."

"I have your permission to tape record you today?"

"Yes, you do."

"Can you tell me in your own words what you know about this accident?"

"I was dispatched to a semi-trailer truck accident involving a pedestrian at about 3:30 am in the 900 block of Pass Highway. When I arrived, a young man flagged me down in a nearby yard."

Gavin stops the officer by raising his hand and asks, "What was the name of that young man?"

"Fred Harris. He told me he just dropped his friend off and his friend, Dean Smith, was walking to his mailbox by the side of the road. The witness saw the semi-trailer drift over the yellow line and strike his friend, knocking him into the next yard, where I found him."

Gavin asks, "Was the mailbox damaged?"

Officer Eaton says, "No. The semi-trailer truck turned sharply at the last second and struck Dean with his right front bumper."

Gavin asks, "What shape did you find Dean Smith in?"

"Very bad shape. I called for an ambulance right away."

Gavin asks, "How long did it take the ambulance to arrive?"

"Less than 4-minutes."

"Did you interview the witness?"

"I tried to, but he was in shock. I had to call for an ambulance for him as well."

"Did you estimate how fast the semi was traveling when he struck Dean Smith?"

"I estimated the speed at 22 mph. That section of the road was under construction and speed was reduced to 25 mph."

"Did you take the statement of the semi-trailer driver at the accident scene?"

"Yes. I spoke to the driver, Andy Davis. He claimed from the beginning he did not cross any yellow line. He claims Dean Smith just stepped in front of him for no reason. He turned sharp left to avoid him, but his right bumper area hit Dean and knocked him into the next yard."

"I see in the accident report that you issued Mr. Davis a ticket for careless driving."

"I did. I did not believe his story of the man suddenly stepping in front of him. I believed the witness and his claim of dropping his friend off to check his mailbox."

Gavin replies, "Anything else about the truck driver or the accident you want to mention in your statement to me?"

Officer Eaton says, "The truck driver kept saying, 'the man stepped out in front of me'."

"Did you ask the truck driver if he was operating his cell phone while driving?"

"Yes, I did. He claims he was not. His eyes were on the road. He almost hit a wild dog a few houses prior and was alert and focused on his driving."

Gavin asks, "Did you ever interview Dean Smith?"

Officer Eaton says, "Yes. The man says the last thing he remembers is walking toward his mailbox."

Gavin asks, "Did you finally interview the witness, Fred Harris?"

Officer Eaton looks at his notes and replies, "A week or so after being treated for shock I went to his residence and spoke to him there."

Gavin asks, "What did Mr. Harris have to say to you?"

Officer Eaton looks at Gavin and replies, "He exited his truck to take a pee and saw the semi-trailer drift over the line and strike his friend."

Gavin turns to Officer Eaton and asks, "Have you ever had a person step in front of a moving semi-trailer truck?"

"Never."

"Are you aware that Dean Smith had been drinking almost the whole night? Fred Harris says Dean was drinking beer from the time they left Dean's residence till their return to Dean's driveway."

"Yes. I found beer cans in Fred Harris's truck after he was transported to the hospital. I also smelled alcohol on Dean Smith's breath when I bent over him at the accident scene. I picked up the results of his blood test at the hospital."

Gavin asks, "What were the results?"

"In Mississippi, legally drunk is .08 and he was .05."

Gavin asks, "Are you aware that Dean Smith was very emotional when he found out his wife had filed for divorce the day before he ran into her at a party?"

"Yes, but so are many other men that love their wives."

Gavin says, "Are you aware Robin gave back her wedding ring to Dean at the party and he wears the wedding ring around his neck?"

"No."

"Did you take any photographs at the scene?"

"No. I wanted to get to the hospital right away to check on Dean Harris. I did go the next day and measure the skid marks of the impact. I also took photographs of the semi-trailer truck's damage."

Gavin says, "This is private investigator Gavin Parker, the time is now 4:08 pm and I am ending the recorded statement at this time."

Officer Eaton turns to Gavin and says, "I hope my recorded statement helps you in your investigation."

"It does, thanks. I was a police officer in Meridian for 18 months".

"Why did you quit?"

"The department went to body cameras and I didn't want to wear one."

Off icer Eaton says, "Our department is talking of getting the cameras."

"What will you do when they do?"

"I don't know. I will worry about it when the department issues the body cameras", says Officer Eaton.

Gavin and Officer Eaton hang-out at the coffee shop about 10 more minutes. They talk about everything except the accident.

Both men stand-up, shake hands and promise to see each other again.

Gavin calls the law office of his client. A few minutes later he is speaking with Attorney Morgan.

"I just took the recorded statement of Officer Eaton. He will make an excellent witness for court."

"Did he say anything that will hurt my settlement chances?"

"Yes. He issued the truck driver a citation for careless driving because he believed Fred Harris and his claim that the plaintiff was walking to his mailbox, when the semi-trailer truck crossed the yellow line and hit the man."

"I am not surprised. No one believes my client when he claims the plaintiff just stepped in front of him without warning."

"One thing that helps your case is the plaintiff drinking beer the whole night. Dean even had a final beer before walking towards his mailbox."

"What was his alcohol level?"

"The officer told me it was .5."

"That is close to being drunk," says Attorney Morgan.

Gavin says, "Robin gave Dean back her wedding ring at the party. She said she filed for divorce. Dean wears Robin's wedding ring around his neck."

Attorney Morgan says, "Interesting about the ring, what are your plans now?"

"I plan to visit the host of the party and locate more witnesses."

"Good. Give me an update tomorrow after 1 pm. I will be out of the office till then."

"Will do. Speak to you tomorrow afternoon."

Both men say goodbye.

Fred Harris drives over to the residence of his best friend, Dean Smith, and rings the doorbell.

Mr. Smith opens the front door and smiles. "What brings you by, Fred? Dean is taking his daily nap."

"I know he is, sir. I came to speak to you."

"Let us go on the back patio. Can I offer you something to drink or eat?"

"No. I am trying to drop 10 pounds."

"Good for you. This way."

Mr. Smith points to a lounge chair by the pool and motions for his star witness to have a seat.

"Do you need more money?"

"No. The $10,000 you gave me is in my bank account. I am here to tell you I gave a statement to a private investigator about your son. Here is his business card."

Bill Harris looks at the business card of Gavin Parker, Parker Investigations, and says, "What did you say in your statement to him?"

"Just like we agreed a few months ago. I told him I was taking a pee by the tree and saw the semi-trailer truck drift across the line and strike your son while walking toward his mailbox."

"Good. You are my star witness. I need the money from the lawsuit to take care of Dean. If we receive millions, like our lawyer believes we will, you will get a few hundred thousand dollars."

"My secret is our secret, sir. Dean is my best friend. We have been pals since 3rd grade. I will protect him, no matter what. Have you discussed the accident with your son?"

Bill Smith says, "Yes. He remembers walking toward his mailbox only."

Fred says, "He doesn't remember stepping in front of the semi-trailer truck on purpose after telling me, 'If Robin doesn't want me, I don't want to live'?"

Bill Smith answers, "No, and I am glad he doesn't remember wanting to take his own life."

"I just can't believe your son lived. That semi-trailer truck was going about 25 mph when Dean stupidly stepped in front of it going down the highway."

Bill Smith looks sad as he replies, "He has always been crazy in love with that woman. She never has called to see how my son is doing."

"What your son, my best friend sees in Robin I do not know."

Bill Smith asks, "Did you mention to the private investigator that my son had been drinking beer all night prior to the accident?"

"Yes, just like we talked about. Stick to our story of the semi-trailer truck crossing the highway line and striking your son, instead of Dean stepping in front of the semi."

Bill Smith smiles and says, "Good. My lawyer, Joe Canton, says he hopes to settle this case in a few months. Your statement to the private investigator made the case one step closer to a settlement."

Fred replies, "Our secret is safe. I want Dean to receive millions as well."

"His mom and I could sure use the settlement money. We plan to hire a full-time nurse."

Fred asks, "Has his new electric wheelchair come in yet?"

Bill Smith replies, "It will be here sometime this week. I received an email from the company yesterday. I like that the chair folds up and fits in the trunk of our Cadillac."

"Remember, I want to come over more."

Bill Smith answers, "I know you do, but it is best you keep your distance till we receive the settlement money."

"I feel bad about the night of the incident."

Bill Smith says, "You keep saying that."

"I do, sir. If I escorted Dean to your front door, he would be 100 percent normal and not the quadriplegic he is."

"Maybe and maybe not. Dean was an emotional wreck from day 1, when Robin mentioned she planned to file for divorce. Then he became an emotional wreck for sure the night of the party, when Robin told him she did file for divorce and gave him back her wedding ring."

Fred asks, "Is the divorce final?"

"Yes. Our son was legally single 2 weeks ago. I am glad he has a huge memory loss with the accident. He doesn't recall being married, meeting her at the party, stepping in front of the semi, nothing."

Fred asks, "Where is Robin living?"

"We do not know. We believe out West. She has family out West."

"Good. The farther away the better. We don't need her nose butting in."

"I agree, but my lawyer says the insurance company will need to take Robin's deposition before any settlement can be final."

Fred says, "I guess my deposition will happen then as well."

"Yes. My lawyer, Joe Canton, will call you very soon. He needs to go over your deposition and what your testimony will be. Just stick to you taking a pee by the tree and seeing the semi-trailer truck drift across the highway line striking Dean and the settlement will happen."

Fred nods his head up and down and asks, "Any settlement offers yet?"

"Yes. The insurance lawyer, Attorney Morgan, offered us $5 million a few weeks ago."

"What did your lawyer say to that offer?"

"He just laughed over the phone when the offer came in. We are demanding $20 million. Our lawyer, Joe Canton, said if the insurance company keeps playing games over the money, we will raise the demand to $30 million."

Fred says, "My Uncle Leo is a financial planner. Maybe you should reach out to him. Too many people spend their lotto winnings and are broke a few years later."

Bill Smith replies, "We have a financial planner already. Eva's brother is with a huge company in California. Most of the money will go towards long-term nursing care. There are no federal taxes taken out on any insurance settlement."

"I didn't know that. That saves you money right there."

Bill Smith says, "With the settlement money, Eva can quit her night job as a cashier at Wal Mart and focus on our son."

Fred says, "And you?"

"I need to work. Being home drives me crazy. I need to keep my mind busy."

Fred looks at Bill Smith and asks, "Do you plan to stay a warehouse manager?"

"Yes. Working with my loyal crew is like family."

"Not me. I plan to travel around the world."

Bill Smith says, "You don't want to remain in college, Fred?"

"I hate sitting in class. I only attend now because my parents pay for my car and rent."

"I will be right back. I want a glass of ice-tea," says Bill Smith leaving the patio for the kitchen.

Fred's telephone rings.

"Hello?"

"Fred, this is attorney Joe Canton. I represent Bill and Eva Smith in their lawsuit against the truck company. We last spoke a few months ago."

"Yes, I remember our conversation back then."

"I just got off the telephone with Attorney Morgan, the insurance lawyer, and he wants to take your deposition next week."

Fred says, "Yes, sir."

"I need for you to come see me this afternoon so I can prepare you."

"Yes, sir."

"How about 4:45 pm?"

"That works for me."

"My office is right next door to Sunshine Mall on Highway 10."

"I will see you at 4:45 pm," says Fred as he watches Mr. Smith return to the patio."

"I just received a call from your attorney."

"Really. What did he have to say?"

Fred says, "He wants me in his office at 4:45 pm today to prepare me for my upcoming deposition."

"Things are moving fast on our lawsuit. That is great. We may be settling soon."

Fred says, "I have never given anyone a deposition in my life."

"They are easy. Just be honest with every question they ask. Just lie when asked 'Did you see the truck driver, drift across the line and strike Dean walking towards his mailbox'?"

Fred looks worried, "I hope they believe me when I say,' I did see the driver drift across the line and strike Dean walking towards his mailbox'."

"The lawyers will believe you because who steps in front of a moving semi-trailer truck? No one does."

Fred looks at Bill Smith and says, "Dean did."

"I know my son did, but there are no eyewitnesses or CCTV cameras to show he did. It comes down to you and your testimony. You are my star witness. Just say you exited your car to take a pee and saw the semi-trailer truck drift across the line and strike Dean walking up to his mailbox."

Fred smiles and says, "I can do that. I want Dean to receive the settlement money, so he can have all the care he needs."

"Good. Just relax, look the lawyers in the eye and answer all their questions. Stick to our secret about the semi-trailer truck drifting across the line and striking my son."

Fred says, "I will call you after I leave the lawyer's office and let you know how my meeting went."

"Great. Dean should be up from his nap. Let us go visit my son."

"Fine with me."

Both walk into Dean's bedroom and view the young man sitting up in bed. He smiles when he sees his dad and Fred walk in.

"Hi Dean, how is my best friend doing today?"

"Everyday is a struggle. My parents have a hard time placing me in my chair."

Fred gives Dean a hug and sits in a chair next to Dean.

"Your dad says your new electric wheelchair will be here sometime this week. Then you can ride in style."

Bill Smith leaves his son's room, giving both men privacy.

Dean turns his head and looks Fred in the eyes. "I remember laying in the grass hurt."

"So little by little your memory is returning?"

Dean says, "Yes. That is all I remember."

Fred looks at his best friend and says, "I saw the semi-trailer truck drift across the highway line and hit you."

"What was I doing by the highway?"

"You exited my car to check your mailbox for your mail. I exited the car to take a leak and saw the truck drift across the highway line and strike you."

Dean says, "My mind is blank."

"Good. It was awful to see. You don't want to remember, believe me."

"Do you want to have lunch? Mom is making hamburgers."

"Not today. I must meet with your lawyer at 4:45 pm. The insurance company will be taking my deposition soon and your lawyer wants to discuss your accident."

Dean asks, "Can you wheel me into the kitchen? I like watching my mother cook."

Fred calls Bill Smith and together they lift Dean out of bed and place him in his wheelchair.

Fred pushes his best friend into the kitchen. He sees Eva flipping hamburgers.

Fred says, "Smells good."

"Want to stay for dinner? I have plenty of hamburger meat."

"I can't today Mrs. Smith. I have to be somewhere at 4:45 pm."

"Please call me, Eva."

"Your lawyer wants to go over my upcoming deposition, Eva."

"My husband and I are counting on you. We need the settlement money."

Dean motions for Eva to step into the dining room, away from Dean.

"I know you do. I will make sure I stick to my story of seeing the semi-trailer truck drift across the highway line and strike your son walking to the mailbox."

"Our lawyer believes the insurance company will give in to our demand and will settle close to our demand price."

"I think so too. If the jury has a heart and they see the condition your son is in, they might reward Dean even more money than your demand."

"The jury might, but we want to move on with our life now."

"I am glad to know your son has no recollection of the incident."

"Me too. He is dealing with enough drama as it is."

"I have to leave now. It is close to 4:30 pm and I want to be on time for my meeting with your lawyer."

"Thanks for being there for us, Fred."

"You welcome. See you all later."

Fred walks back into the kitchen and says goodbye to his best friend.

Fred exits the residence, enters his truck, and departs the neighborhood.

Fred slowly drives over to the law firm and waits in their parking lot.

At 4:40 pm Fred Harris walks into the law office and says to the receptionist, "Afternoon. I have a 4:45 pm appointment with Attorney Joe Canton."

The female receptionist asks, "Your name, sir?"

"Fred Harris."

"My boss told me to place you in our conference room. Follow me. Care for something to drink?"

"A bottle of water if you have one."

"We do."

Fred is escorted to the large conference room and takes a seat.

"I will be right back with your water."

Fred says, "Thank you."

Attorney Joe Canton walks in with a file in his hands and closes the door behind him.

"We finally meet in person."

"Yes sir."

"Call me, Joe."

"Yes sir, I mean Joe."

The receptionist knocks on the closed door.

"Come in."

The receptionist hands Fred his cold bottle of water, exits the conference room, and closes the door behind her.

Joe opens his file marked 'Dean Smith VS Silver Streak Freight Forwarders and says, "Your deposition will be on Monday at 11 am right here in this room."

"Can I have a sheet of paper and a pen to write it down?"

"I will give you a printed schedule sheet just before you depart my law office."

"Thank you, Joe."

"Come wearing a shirt and slacks combo and have a fresh haircut too."

Fred says, "I will do that, no problem."

"The defense will be asking many questions, just answer all of them as truthfully as you can. If you do not understand the question presented, just look over at me and say, 'I don't understand the question'."

Fred again says, "I can do that, no problem."

"I will have the defense attorney ask the question again in a different way so you will understand. Do not answer any question asked right away. Wait 5 seconds, giving me time to object. Can you do that?"

Fred looks at the lawyer and says, "I can do that, no problem."

"The questions will start slowly with your name, address, who you live with, occupation, education level, any military, married or single, things like that. The defense lawyer will finally get around to the night of the violent impact. Again, listen to each question, wait 5 seconds, giving me time to object if I need to before you answer."

Fred nods up and down and says, "Simple enough."

"The key things the defense will want to know are: the amount of drinking my client did that night, his relationship with his ex-wife, how did he react to his wife saying we are getting a divorce, to what my client's actions were when exiting your vehicle, to the time he was struck by the semi-trailer truck. The defense lawyer will ask you many questions about the actions of the semi-truck trailer driver, him crossing the line, where you were, what you were doing, what my client was doing, things like that."

"I will pay attention, wait 5 seconds before answering any questions and I will be a good witness for Dean."

"I took your phone statement a few months ago. Let me go over the statement now to make sure things have not changed. Dean drank beer all night, first at your residence, then in the truck, then at the party his ex-wife was at, then a final beer in his own driveway before being struck. He was not drunk but could stand and walk on his own. He exited your truck in his driveway to check his mailbox for any mail. You exited the truck to take a pee by a tree and that is when you saw the semi-trailer truck slowly drift across the line and strike Dean. You saw Dean fly into the next yard, and you thought he was dead. You felt bad you did not escort Dean to his front door, and you know the truck driver is at fault for this accident. We discussed Dean wearing dark clothing and was hard to see walking to his mailbox."

"That is all correct, Joe."

"Good. Just stick to the same answers when the defense attorney asks them. Once he is finished, I will have a few more questions to ask, then we will be finished. Just make sure you do not speak to anyone between now and the deposition and do not give any statements to anyone. Send them to me."

Fred says, "I gave a statement today to a private investigator hired by Attorney Morgan."

"What did you say to him and was it recorded?"

"Yes, it was recorded. I told him the truck driver crossed the line and struck Dean by the mailbox."

"Good. No more statements to no one. Have them come see me."

"I will do that."

"One more thing. Mr. and Mrs. Smith did not pay you any money to be a witness. You came forward on your own."

Fred says, "I came forward because I saw the semi strike my good friend and I wanted the truth to come out."

"Good answer. Stay away from Dean and his family till after we settle. I want the defense to see you as a witness and not as Dean's buddy."

Fred says, "I will not go over anymore or make phone calls to the dad, nothing."

"Good. I think once they take your deposition and I take the depositions of their traffic expert, and a half-dozen other people, we will settle. I do not see this going to trial. The jury would eat them alive once they see Dean being pushed into the courtroom."

Fred says," I cannot believe my friend survived being stuck by a semi-trailer truck."

Joe responds, "All the alcohol in his system made his body go limp."

"I am ready for my deposition."

"Good to hear. Just be yourself, look everyone in the eye when you speak, and you will do fine. The police officer on scene issued the truck driver a ticket for careless driving. Then you seeing the driver crossing the highway all help your friend's case. I bet the truck driver has a bad habit of driving and looking at his cell phone at the same time. Let me walk you out."

By the front door of the law firm, Joe hands Fred his deposition time typed-up and says, "Come see me 30 minutes prior, will you?"

Fred says "Sure, no problem. I wanted to tell you one more thing,"

"What is it?"

"At the party on Saturday night, Robin stood up and handed Dean her wedding ring and said she filed for divorce just a day earlier. He cried like a baby in the host's restroom too. He wears Robin's wedding ring around his neck."

"Sounds like I have a very emotional client."

Both men shake hands and Fred exits the building.

Fred calls Bill Smith at his residence.

"Hi Bill. My interview went off without a hitch. I like Joe Canton. He told me no more contact with your family till after he settles your case."

"I understand Fred. It won't be long, maybe a few months longer."

"I agree. I hope Dean improves daily."

"Me too. Take care and thanks for calling."

"No problem, bye."

Gavin drives back to his office to run data to locate Robin Smith.

He types in the same address as Dean's into the system. The data shows an address of 330 Casino Boulevard in Las Vegas, Nevada. Gavin researches the Las Vegas address and finds out it comes back to the Clark County Detention Center.

Gavin looks up the telephone number for the jail and speaks with a Deputy. Gavin confirms the woman was in jail for a shoplifting offense but was released a month ago. The deputy gives Gavin the bonding company and phone number. Gavin dials the telephone number.

A female says on the 3rd ring, "Quick Release Bail Bonds."

Gavin identifies himself as a private investigator in Gulfport, Mississippi and explains he is trying to locate a Robin Smith.

The female gives Gavin an emergency contact phone number for Robin that she listed when released on bond. The bonding office says Robin showed-up in court, pled guilty and was fined 2,000 dollars and spent a week behind bars.

Gavin thanks the woman, hangs up and dials the number she provided. It just rings and rings and no one answers. Gavin looks up the area code, 253, and it shows the area code is for Tacoma, Washington.

Gavin turns his computer off and falls asleep in the portable cot he keeps in his small office.

A few hours later Gavin wakes from his nap and heats up a cup of coffee. He then tries the Tacoma number again. This time a female picks up and says, "Hello?"

"My name is Gavin Parker, a private investigator in Gulfport, Mississippi. Can I speak with Robin Smith please?"

"This is her Sister, Sharon. She is not at this number. Why do you want to speak with my younger sister for?"

"I need her to come back to Gulfport to give her deposition regarding Dean Smith."

"Robin is not working and hasn't the money to fly out to Gulfport."

"The insurance company's defense lawyer will pay all her expenses to travel to Gulfport and will fly her back to Tacoma."

"Let me have your number, Gavin. I will call my sister and ask if she wants to talk to you. I can not promise she will call you."

"No problem. It is area code 228, and the phone number is 224-7659. Please tell her I am willing to pay all her expenses to come back to Gulfport, Airfare, food, lodging, whatever she needs."

"I will tell her, but again, I can not promise Robin will call you."

Gavin asks, "Your mother lives in Gulfport, right?"

'No. My mom lives in Ocean Springs."

"I understand. I am hoping she wants to visit her mom while here in Mississippi. I will rent her a car or if she wants, I can also drive her there myself, but I need her here in Gulfport soon."

Sharon asks, "Can I come too?"

"No problem."

"I will call Robin to ring you back. We can visit our mother together."

"Thank you," says Gavin and hangs up his cell phone.

Gavin looks at his watch. The time is 7pm. He figures it must be 5pm in Tacoma.

Gavin changes clothes and has another cup of coffee. His cell phone rings, and the caller ID shows Tacoma as the area code.

"This is Gavin Parker."

"This is Robin Meade, my sister asked me to call you."

Gavin says, "Thanks for calling me back. Is Meade your maiden name?"

"Yes."

"I told your sister I will pay all expenses for you and for her to travel to and from Gulfport. I will rent you both a car to visit your mother in Ocean Springs, or I can drive you anywhere you need to go. The insurance company needs to take your deposition regarding Dean's accident.

"I can do that. When will this deposition take place?"

"I have to contact my client, the insurance defense law firm of Morgan and Rodgers to see it up. I will do that now and then I will call you back."

"I am not giving anyone my home address or cell phone number. Arrange for my travel via my older sister. I can travel anytime you need."

"Good. I will call your sister soon. Thanks for calling me back."

"You welcome."

Both say goodbye to each other.

Gavin calls the law firm of Morgan and Rodgers. The time is now 8:30 pm.

An operator comes on and says, "This is the answering service for Morgan and Rodgers, "How can I help you tonight?"

"This is Gavin Parker. I am trying to reach attorney Morgan, my client."

"There is a note by my computer screen, sir. It says to call attorney Morgan at any hour if you call. What is your phone number? I will have attorney Morgan call you."

"My cell is area code 228-224-7659."

" Do you need anything else from me at this time?"

Gavin says, "No."

"I will call attorney Morgan now. Have a good night, sir."

Gavin says, "You too" and hangs up.

A minute or so later Gavin's cell phone rings.

"This is Gavin."

"Hello Gavin, Attorney Morgan here. What is going on with my case?"

"I located Robin. She is living in Tacoma, Washington and is willing to travel to Gulfport on 2 conditions."

Attorney Morgan asks, "What are the 2 conditions?"

"Robin wants her older sister, named Sharon, to come too. Robin wants you to rent-a-car so she can travel to Ocean Springs to visit her mother."

"Great. This is an important case. I need you to fly to Tacoma and escort them back to Gulfport. I want you to rent them a nice hotel room, stay with them till the deposition is taken, then rent them a car and escort them back to the Gulfport airport to fly out. Can you do that for me?"

"Yes, I can."

Attorney Morgan says, "I want you to buy her a nice dress and shoes, get her hair cut, a facial, the works. I want her looking beautiful for her deposition. I need you to also rent a hotel room next door to her. Stay with the 2 women till the deposition is over."

"I can do that. How do I pay for all this?"

"Come by my law office. I will give you a company credit card and 2 thousand cash."

Gavin asks, "What amount am I aloud to charge on the law firm credit card?"

Attorney Morgan laughs and replies, "No set limit. Just get Robin Smith to Gulfport. I will have the date of her deposition in the morning. Have her in Gulfport a few days earlier so I can meet with her."

Gavin says, "No problem. I will come by your office around 9 am."

"Good. Anything else?"

Gavin says, Yes, Robin is now using her maiden name of Meade. She spent about a week in jail for shoplifting in Las Vegas, Nevada last month."

"No big deal. Minor offense. Thanks for telling me. See you in the morning."

"I will see you then."

Both men say goodbye and hang up.

Gavin calls back Sharon.

"Hello?"

"Hi, Sharon. This is Gavin in Gulfport. Do you have a minute to talk?"

"Yes, go ahead."

"I spoke to my attorney and it is a 'go' for you both to fly to Gulfport. I will know in the morning the date of your sister's deposition. Once I know, I will call you back, regarding your travel schedule. My client wants me to fly to Tacoma and escort you both to Gulfport."

"Wow, really?"

"Yes. Your sister is an important witness for my client, and he wants to make sure she arrives for her deposition."

"I understand."

"I will put you both up at the downtown Hilton, buy you nice dresses, arrange for a beauty makeover, the works at no cost. I also will give you 500 dollars each in cash to have spending money for your stay. Once the deposition is over, I will rent the car you will need to travel to Ocean Springs. I don't mind being your driver if you want."

"Alright. I will wait for your call in the morning."

"Any problem with getting off work?"

"I work from home, so I will just bring my laptop with me and work from the Hilton."

"Great. What about Robin? I understand she is not working."

"Correct. I am paying her living expenses for a few months. She might enroll in our community college."

"Good for you for helping your sister. I will call you back as soon as I hear from my client. It should be by noon tomorrow."

"I will be standing by," says Sharon.

They both say goodbye.

James Paul Ellison

DAY 3 – THURSDAY

Thursday morning at 9:00 am, Gavin calls the law firm of Morgan and Rodgers.

"Morning, Morgan and Rodgers Law Firm. How can I assist you?"

"Morning to you, Cindy. This is your favorite private investigator Gavin Parker."

Cindy laughs and says, "You are the only private investigator I know."

Gavin response, "Good to hear. Can I speak with Attorney Morgan?"

"Not this morning. He is in a deposition since 9 am. He told me to tell you the deposition of Robin Smith or Robin Meade is this Sunday, here in our conference room at 11 am. He wants you to bring Robin to his office at 10 am for their meeting. There is an envelope here at my desk for you containing cash and a credit card."

"Alright, I just made a note of her deposition in my calendar. I am on my way for the envelope." says Gavin.

Cindy says, "Pray for me. I am up for a raise."

Gavin says, "I will pray every night."

Cindy says, "When I was 14 years old, I lived in Gig Harbor, just across the bridge from Tacoma. I loved seeing Mount McKinley every day when walking to the school bus."

Gavin says, "This will be my first trip out West. I am looking forward to going."

Cindy says, "Please bring me a coffee cup from Gig Harbor."

Gavin answers, "Will do. I have to say goodbye. I need to book my flight to Seattle. Talk to you later. Have a great day."

Cindy says, "Will try. Have a safe flight."

Gavin calls Sharon in Tacoma.

"Hello?"

"Morning Sharon. This is Gavin in Gulfport."

"Morning. Robin is here doing her laundry. Let me put you on speaker phone. Go ahead."

"Robin your deposition is this Sunday at 11 am. I will fly out tomorrow. Be ready to travel. I will book 3 airline tickets with Delta for Friday afternoon to depart from Seattle. Saturday, we will go shopping for clothes and visit a hair salon. Sunday morning, we will meet with Attorney Morgan and he will go over your deposition   scheduled for an hour later. Monday you can drive to Ocean Springs and visit your mother. I have an open return ticket to Seattle when you are ready to go home. Any questions?"

Robin says, "Tell me who represents my ex-husband?"

"Attorney Morgan represents the semi-truck driver and his employer. Attorney Joe Canton represents Dean. By the way, the Smith family is demanding 20 million dollars. Attorney Morgan already offered 5 million and the family turned it down."

Robin says, "I don't want to see or speak with Dean or his parents."

"I can arranger that", lies Gavin. Let me go. I have to purchase the airline tickets and reserve a rent-a-car."

All 3 say goodbye and hang up.

Gavin contacts Delta Airlines and books his flight to Seattle for later that day. He then books 3 tickets from Seattle to Gulfport, Mississippi with a stop in Dallas. Gavin calls Enterprise and books his rental car for Seattle. Gavin books a rental car for the 2 ladies for next Monday with Enterprise in Gulfport.

Gavin makes himself a cup of tea while he packs a suitcase. He takes a shower. He gets dress, grabs his suitcase and briefcase, and heads out the door. He stops at McDonalds drive-up for a meal, which he eats as he drives to the airport.

Just 30 minutes later Gavin is in the terminal sitting in the departure lounge. His flight will depart on time for Dallas. He has an hour layover before arriving in Seattle 4 hours later.

Gavin checks his weather app for the weather in Seattle and Tacoma. The app says it will be raining upon his arrival.

Gavin is called to board his flight. He sits in first-class by the window. Gavin planned to take a short nap till an extremely attractive woman sits in the aisle seat. Gavin smiles and the woman smiles back. Gavin reaches in his shirt pocket and retrieves his business card.

Gavin hands the woman his calling card and says, "In case you need a private investigator."

The woman laughs and says, "I do need one."

Gavin asks, "Are you a lawyer by chance?"

"No, I own a dress shop in Biloxi. I fired a clerk last week and she stole 4,000 from me and 3 dresses."

Gavin says, "I can locate her for you."

The woman says, "Great. I trusted that ex-employee. I even had her close the shop a few times."

Gavin says, "I would do a complete inventory check of your store, including storage facility. Most criminals when they still a check from their employer, remove the last few checks to use later."

"Good idea. I will do that when I return to my store."

"Who is running the store now while you are traveling?"

"My mother."

Gavin looks at the woman and says, "Do you trust your mother?"

The woman laughs and replies, "With all my heart."

Gavin says, "Good to hear."

The male steward walks down the aisle and says to the passengers, "Please buckle-up."

Gavin and the woman buckle-up and continue to make small talk.

The Delta flight from Gulfport, Mississippi to Dallas, Texas is 1 hour and 20 minutes. The flight takes off at 11:30 am. Once in the air, the steward walks the cabin offering drinks only.

After receiving their cold drinks Gavin asks, "What is your name?"

"Gail Cummings."

"Why are you traveling to Dallas if you don't mind me asking?"

"My dress supplier is there. I want to inspect new dresses they received."

Gavin says, "I am going to Seattle. I am working a case for a local law firm."

"Seattle, that is a long way."

"I know. I located a witness for my law firm client. Now I will escort the woman back to Gulfport for her deposition."

"Sounds like she is an important witness."

"Robin is especially important. It is an ongoing case so I can't discuss the details."

Gail laughs and says, "I understand."

Gavin pulls out a note pad and pen and asks, "What is the name of the ex-employee that stole from you?"

"How much will this cost me?"

Gavin laughs and replies, "No money. Just 1 dress when and if I need to send a friend your way."

Gail smiles and says, "Deal. My ex-employee is Brenda Avery."

"What is her age and last known address?"

"I have it right here in my purse. I was planning to search for her on social media sites during the flight."

"Gavin laughs and says, "You would be wasting your time. I have access to the same data the police use."

Gail says, "Wow. Glad we are sitting in the same row."

"Me too."

Gail gives Gavin her ex-employee's last known address. Gavin types the information into the system and waits. A minute or so later the information pops on the screen of his laptop.

Gavin shows the results to Gail.

"Your ex-employee is currently living at 2339 Elks Road in Bay Saint Louis. Let me also see who lives at that address with her."

Gavin types the Elks Road address into the system. A minute goes by before the information appears on the laptop.

"It looks like a male named Barry Cook, age 26, lives there.

Gail says, "Her boyfriend is named Barry."

Gavin says, "When you return to Biloxi see the police. Give them her address in Bay Saint Louis. The police in that jurisdiction will arrest her. Biloxi police can have her transferred to their jail."

"That simple?"

Gavin looks at Gail and replies, "That simple."

"Wow, that information is worth a dress."

"I have a girl in mind. What are the steps for her to collect the free dress?"

Gail writes a little note and hands it to Gavin.

"Give her this note to hand to one of my clerks."

Gavin opens the note and reads, 'One free dress to person with this note' and it is signed Gail Cummings.

"Thanks," says Gavin placing the note in his wallet.

Gavin says, If, you need me to place your ex-employee under surveillance to see what the woman is up to, just call me?"

Gail says, "I will."

Gavin says, "I would do background checks on all new hires to see if the person has a criminal record before you decide to hire."

Gail sips on her coke and says, "Sound advice. How much is a background check?"

Gavin says, "I charge 75 a check but for you I will only charge 40."

Gail smiles and replies, "I will call you for sure."

Gavin and Gail make small talk till the flight lands in Dallas.

Gail grabs her items and is about to exit when she says, "I hope to give one pretty dress to a nice private investigator soon."

Gavin looks-up at Gail and responds, "I hope I find the right woman to give the gift to."

Gail laughs and says, "Do a background check."

Both laugh and say their goodbyes.

After a few minutes on the ground the steward stops at Gavin's seat and says, "You can wait 30 minutes in the terminal if you like."

Gavin says, "I will try to take a quick nap here in my seat."

The steward replies, "Fine with me, sir. I will not disturb you."

Gavin says, "Thank you" and reclines his seat.

An hour later the steward shakes Gavin's shoulder and says, "You need to sit-up now. We are about to board."

Gavin sits up as people start to fill the cabin. No one occupies Gavin's other 2 seats in first class.

The flight departs 15 minutes late. The captain makes an announcement.

"Hello everyone. This is Captain Joe Norman. The flight should touch down in Seattle in just over 4 hours. We will be serving a hot lunch shortly. On behalf of Delta, I wish you all a pleasant flight."

Gavin retrieves a notepad and pen from his briefcase. At the top of the notepad he writes, 'Thins to do while in Washington'. Gavin makes a numbered list.

1. Coffee cup for Cindy from Gig Harbor

2. Retrieve the rent-a-car.

3. Call Robin and sister to say he landed.

4. Book a hotel in Tacoma for 1 night.

5. Call attorney Morgan to say he is in Washington and update case.

6. Play back office answering machine messages.

7. Visit the Space Needle

8. Ride a ferry over to Gig Harbor.

Gavin then writes, "To do back in Gulfport'.

1. Take women to hotel to check in.

2. Gavin to check in too.

3. Take Robin to buy clothes.

4. Get Robin a haircut and facial.

5. Call Attorney Morgan you are back in Gulfport.

6. Give women 500 dollars each.

7. Rent car after Robin's deposition.

8. Take Robin to visit Attorney Morgan.

9. Take Robin to her deposition.

10. Avoid contact between Robin and Dean.

11. Take Cindy her coffee cup gift and find-out if single.

12. Single or not give Cindy note for free dress.

13. Wash and vacuum car

14. Take in a movie.

15. Place Dean Smith under surveillance

16. Interview Ambulance crew

17. Visit media outlets for any info on accident.

18. Bring time sheet for Attorney Morgan current

The steward arrives with Gavin's hot meal and says, "Care for a glass of wine?"

Gavin nods yes and puts his notepad back into his briefcase.

A few minutes later the steward brings Gavin 2 small bottles of red wine.

Gavin opens the 1st bottle of red wine and pours the contents into a plastic glass on his tray. He takes a sip of wine, then another. Gavin studies the label. The wine is from Spain. The bottle reads '2 Amigos'. Gavin takes another sip of wine, then another.

Gavin looks up at the steward as he pushes the beverage cart by his seat and says, "Thank you for the wine."

The steward says, "My pleasure. Compliments of Delta."

Gavin asks, "What is your name?"

"Matt."

"Here is my business card. I am offering you a free locate anywhere in the USA."

"Matt says, "Wow. Thank you."

"No problem."

Matt continues to push the beverage cart down the aisle.

After the meal trays are collected, Gavin stretches out on the half-full flight and takes a nap.

Matt wakes Gavin up from his deep sleep and says, "We will be landing in 30 minutes."

Gavin yawns and replies, "Your Delta seats are comfortable, I had a good nap."

Matt says, "Can I get you anything?"

Gavin replies, "How about a few bags of your salted peanuts?"

Matt nods and says, "I will be right back."

Gavin is looking out the window at the landscape when the steward brings him a few bags of nuts and a couple of small bottles of wine.

Gavin says, "Thanks. I will save the wine for my hotel room in Tacoma."

The flight lands at 3 pm Seattle time without any problems. The Captain comes on over the p.a. system and says, "Welcome everyone to Seattle. Thank you for flying Delta and I hope we will see you again."

Gavin is one of the first to exit the plane. He heads right over to the luggage area to wait for his one suitcase.

Once Gavin collects his suitcase, he walks a short distance to Enterprise-Rent-a-Car.

After some paperwork, he rides the shuttle to row 4 and locates his Nissan Altima.

First stop is the Space Needle.

Gavin read a pamphlet at the Seattle Airport about the landmark. It opened in April 1962 for the Century 21 Exposition. It took 400 days to build. Over 1.3 million guest a year visit the Space Needle. It cost 4.5 million dollars in 1962 to build. That amount today is 100 million dollars.

Gavin sits in his rental car and rereads the pamphlet. The Space Needle is privately owned. The monument stands 605 feet, offers a 360-degree view, and takes 43 seconds to travel up the elevator to the top.

Gavin departs the airport for downtown Seattle. Traffic is heavy on Highway I-5. The GPS in the car says he will arrive in 30 minutes. Gavin is excited and cannot wait to visit the Space Needle.

The parking lot is full when Gavin arrives. The line to purchase a ticket is long as well. To save time Gavin walks up to a family of 4 near the front of the line and says, "I will purchase your tickets if I can buy a ticket for me. I am in a rush."

The man says, "We waited 40 minutes to get to this point. Sure, you have a deal."

Gavin stands with the family talking to them like he is a family member. Ten minutes later they reach the purchase window. Gavin turns to the man and says, "Tell the cashier the type of tickets you want."

The man looks at the different choices and says, "We want the Space Needle, Chihuly Garden and Glass Combination ticket."

Gavin then says to the cashier, "I want the 20-minute Space Needle narrated scenic tour and I am paying for my brother's family and my ticket."

The agent behind the glass says, "The two adults are 50 dollars each, the children are 25 dollars each and your ticket is 30 dollars. Your total with tax is 194.80."

Gavin hands the agent his Visa card.

The tickets are handed to Gavin.

Gavin hands the man his 4 tickets, winks, and says, "Well, brother, enjoy your tour."

The happy man winks back and says, "Enjoy your 20-minute narrative tour."

The men shake hands and Gavin walks inside the Space Needle.

A large sign directs Gavin where to wait for the next tour. A small group of military men, in uniform soon join him.

Gavin turns to the 5 and says, "Thanks for your military service."

The men and Gavin make small talk till a middle-aged woman in a blue uniform arrives. "My name is Donna. I will be your narrator. Follow me to the elevator."

Once inside, Donna says, "We only have 20-minutes. I want to give you plenty of time to walk around the 360-degree observation deck."

As they exit the elevator, Donna points to a massive high fence surrounding the Space Needle and says, "Following 2 suicides in 1974, we added the improved fence and netting beneath the observation deck. After everything was installed, we had a female commit suicide in July 1975. This is when we hired additional security staff to stay on the observation deck during operational hours."

Gavin looks around the observation deck and sees no security guards in uniform. He says to Donna, "I see no uniform guards."

Donna looks at Gavin and replies, "The guards are plain clothes and hired to blend in with the crowd. We have several attempted suicides a year."

Donna points to a white-capped mountain in the distance and says, "This is Denali, 20,310 feet in height. The mountain was named, Mount McKinley."

Gavin pulls out of his pocket a small camera and asks, "Can you take a picture of me with Denali behind me, please?"

Gavin hands his Canon camera to Donna. He stands there and smiles as Donna snaps a few photos.

Donna asks Gavin, "Where are you from?"

"I am from Gulfport, Mississippi."

Donna laughs and says, "I was in your town last month on a casino junket. I lost 600 dollars."

Gavin replies, Thanks for your donation to our economy. From here I will take a ferry to Bremerton. I have to go to Gig Harbor to buy a coffee cup for a friend that used to live in that town."

Donna reaches into her large bag she is carrying and pulls out a flyer on the ferry to Bremerton. "The Puget Sound Naval Shipyard is a popular tourist destination as well."

"From Gig Harbor, my final stop is a hotel in Tacoma."

Donna says, "Seattle to Bremerton by ferry is an hour, Bremerton to Gig Harbor by car is 20 minutes and from Gig to Tacoma over the Narrows Bridge is 25 minutes."

"Gavin writes this all down on a small notepad he always carries in his back pocket. "Thanks, Donna for the helpful information."

"You welcome."

Donna hands Gavin a business card for the ferry terminal in Seattle. "Just go to 801 Alaskan Way Pier 52. The ferry departs every 30 minutes. This ferry carries people and cars. Pier 50 carries people and bicycles, so make sure you go to pier 52."

Gavin takes the business card and says, "I will."

Donna says to Gavin, "Let us rejoin the group."

A few minutes later Donna says to her people, "Where do you plan to have dinner?"

One of the military men says, Chinook's. They serve American and seafood."

Donna replies, "Correct, plus fresh off the boat."

Gavin laughs and says, "I am having Subway. I am in a rush."

The group of men start asking Donna about different tourist attractions. Gavin hands Donna a 20-dollar tip, waves goodbye and leaves. He walks around the 360-degree observation deck snapping a few photos along the way.

Gavin exits the Space Needle and departs the area.

Gavin arrives at Pier 52 and parks his car on the departing ferry. He finds a seat inside and starts making phone calls.

Gavin calls Sharon in Tacoma but gets her answering machine. "This is Gavin. I am in town. I will call back in the morning."

Gavin calls the law firm of Morgan and Rodgers. A male comes on and says, "This is the answering service for the law firm of Morgan and Rodgers."

Gavin says, "This is private investigator Parker. I have 2 messages. The first message is for Cindy. I am in Gig Harbor picking up your coffee cup. The 2nd message is for Attorney Morgan. I will be in a Tacoma hotel tonight. I plan to meet with your witness in the morning."

The male operator responds, "Very good, sir. I will pass on both messages."

Gavin says, "Thank you" and hangs up.

Gavin puts his cell phone away and watches the ferry crew prepare to depart pier 52.

For the next hour Gavin watches the ferry cross the Puget Sound He takes in the mountains and bay views. He watches the homes along the shoreline. He takes out his Canon camera and snaps a few photos.

The p.a. system comes on.

"This is Captain Hicks. Welcome aboard the ferry name 'Kalestan'. Our arrival time in Bremerton is just over an hour. The snack bar is now open. Thank you for taking our ferry this afternoon."

Gavin goes to the snack bar and buys a hot cup of coffee and a bag of cookies. He stands by a rail on the 2nd deck and takes in the breathtaking views.

The ferry lands in Bremerton. A short while later Gavin is back in his rental car. He drives straight into downtown Gig Harbor. He wants to make sure he can purchase a coffee cup before the shops close.

Gavin stops at Kimball Coffeehouse at 6659 Kimball Drive. There are hundreds of coffee mugs on shelving lining the walls. Gavin buys a coffee and starts browsing the many cups he can choose from.

Gavin decides on a Gig Harbor Evening Reflection coffee mug. Th cup says, 'Welcome to Gig Harbor' with an image of a mountain and boats in the harbor. Gavin buys 2 at 15 dollars each. He instructs the friendly clerk to wrap them well. He exits the store a happy man.

Gavin stops at a Subway Restaurant nearby and orders a footlong Ham sandwich to go. Gavin then drives over the Narrows Bridge into Tacoma. He finds the downtown Hilton without a problem. Gavin is soon in his room on the 5th floor. He eats his sandwich and is so tired, falls asleep on top of the bed in his clothes.

DAY 4 – FRIDAY

On Friday morning Gavin wakes up at 7 am. He takes a shower, gets dressed and exits the Hilton. He sits in his rental car and calls Sharon and Robin.

Sharon answers, "Hello?"

"Morning Sharon. This is Gavin. Ready for breakfast?"

"We are. Where at?"

"Denny's, one block from the downtown Hilton where I stayed last night."

"Sure, what time?"

Gavin says, "How about now?"

"We are ready. Meet you there in 15 minutes. I will be carrying a big brown purse."

"Great. I will go there now and reserve our table."

"Great. What time is our flight?"

"We depart on Delta at noon."

Sharon says, "We must leave Tacoma by 10:00 am. Traffic sometimes is heavy."

Gavin asks, "You ladies are ready, right?"

"Yes. We can have a quick breakfast and then go straight to the airport."

Gavin says, "Do you need me to pick you 2 up?"

Sharon replies, "No. My boyfriend is going to have breakfast with us, then go back home."

Gavin asks, "His name?"

"Mark. I will pay for his meal."

Gavin laughs and says, "No. The law firm I work for will."

Sharon says, "I like saving money. Thanks. See you soon. What do you look like?"

Gavin says, "I will be wearing a blue Gig Harbor ball cap I bought."

Sharon replies, "We are leaving my house now."

Gavin says, "Perfect. I am parking at Denny's now."

Sharon says goodbye and hangs up her cell phone.

Gavin walks into Denny's and asks for a quiet table by a window.

The hostess asks, "How many in your party?"

Gavin answers, "There are 4 of us."

The hostess walks over to a corner table for 6. "Will this do?"

Gavin replies, "Perfect."

The hostess looks at Gavin and says, "I like your ball cap. The color matches your eyes." She puts down the menus and says, "Sally, your waitress, will be right with you."

Gavin looks out toward the parking lot when his waitress walks up and says, "Good morning, Sir."

"Morning."

"Do you want to order a beverage while you wait for the others?"

"Yes. Coffee with cream and sugar."

An old Chevy truck pulls into the parking lot. Gavin watches 3 people exit. They are 2 women and a man. One is carrying a large brown purse.

They walk into the restaurant and start to look around. Gavin stands up and waves his blue ball cap. They walk over.

Gavin asks, "Are you Sharon and Robin?"

The women smile and reply, "Yes."

Gavin looks at the young man and says, "You must be Mark?"

"Yes."

Gavin says, "Have a seat. You must be hungry?"

They all nod their heads.

Gavin looks at the younger woman and asks, "Are you, Robin?"

She smiles and says, "Yes. I am."

Gavin says to all 3 as they sit down, "We will not talk about the accident in Gulfport."

Robin nods and says, "I would like that."

Gavin replies, "Consider it done."

The waitress walks over with Gavin's coffee and asks, "What do you 3 want to drink?"

The waitress takes their drink orders and walks away.

Gavin says, "Everything is on my law firm client's credit card, so have whatever you want."

Mark laughs and says, "Good to hear."

Sharon says, "I see you bought a Gig Harbor ball cap."

Gavin takes the ball cap off and replies, I also bought a Dallas, Tacoma, and a Seattle one."

Robin says, "You must like ball caps to buy so many."

Gavin laughs and says, "I don't normally wear them. When away from Gulfport, I buy a cap as a reminder of where I have been."

The waitress returns with the beverages. "Are you all ready to order?"

Gavin raises his hand and replies, "Give me the check, please."

The waitress nods and says, "No problem, sir."

After everyone places their orders Gavin says to Robin, "You like Washington State?"

"No. It rains too much. No sun gets me depressed."

Sharon speaks next.

"I told my sister, give it a few more months. It takes a while to get used to walking around with clouds hiding the sun."

Mark replies, "I was born in Tacoma. I love this weather. Not like Florida, hot all the time. My sister lives in Miami and hates visiting me. I have to travel there if I want to see her."

Gavin asks, "When was the last time you visited your sister?"

Mark thinks for a minute and replies, "3 years next month."

Robin asks Gavin, "You like being a private investigator?"

"I do very much. I love doing surveillances. Every day is different with a claimant."

Mark says, "You call a person, claimant?"

Gavin replies, "I have many insurance clients and they call the person claimant. I just follow along."

The waitress returns with a full pot of coffee. "Anyone care for a refill?"

Gavin hands his cup to the waitress and says, "Sure."

The waitress fills his cup and says, "I just checked with the kitchen. Your 4 orders are next."

Mark rubs his stomach and says, "My unlimited pancake order will be my main meal today."

Sharon says to Gavin, "My boyfriend is trying to drop some weight."

Gavin laughs and says, "Pancakes have a high number of calories once you add in the syrup and butter."

Mark says, "I will start a new diet tomorrow."

Everyone laughs at Mark's answer.

The waitress and a helper bring the group their orders. She says, "Anything missing or is there anything you need?"

Gavin speaks up. "The ketchup is missing, and we need more sugar."

"I will be right back with the items."

Sharon turns to Gavin and asks, "Did you go sightseeing in Seattle?"

"I did. I took a quick tour of the Space Needle."

Sharon replies, "I am afraid of heights."

Gavin looks at her and asks, "What about the flight?"

"I will just close my eyes the whole time."

Gavin says, "We are talking about 4 hours to Dallas and another hour from there to Gulfport."

Sharon replies, "I will close my eyes the whole trip."

Gavin looks at Robin as she cuts her ham and asks, "What about you? Are you afraid of heights?"

Robin says, "No. I wish I was a stewardess."

Gavin says, "Then apply with all the major airlines."

"I have. I am just waiting for answers."

Sharon replies, "The airlines take forever to say yes or no."

Mark speaks up. "That is the truth."

Gavin looks at Mark and asks, "What do you do for a job?"

"I am a warehouse manager for a shipping company."

Gavin asks, "How long have you been doing that?"

"It is my dad's company. I started work right after high school. So almost 9 years."

Gavin looks at Sharon and asks, "What type of work are you in?

"I clean houses."

Gavin looks at Robin and asks, "What do you do for a living?"

"Nothing. I am going from company to company applying and interviewing."

Mark looks at Gavin and asks, "How did you get in the private investigative business?"

"I was a policeman in Meridian, Mississippi for 18 months, then decided to go on my own. Almost all private investigators are ex-law enforcement."

Mark asks, "Why did you quit a good paying job?"

"The department went to body cameras. I did not want to be judged one day for my actions on the street. Too many policemen around the nation get jammed up that way."

Robin says, "I agree with you, Gavin."

"With being my own boss, I have flexible hours. I just do not have a steady paycheck. I am at the mercy of the telephone ringing."

Mark asks, "Do you get paid to travel to Tacoma and back to Gulfport?"

"I do. I charge a lower rate to travel or to sleep in a hotel, but all my hours are billable."

Mark laughs and replies, "That sounds like the job for me. How do I become a private investigator in Washington State?"

Gavin says, "I do not know. Every state is different. Google Division of Licensing in your state and read the rules. Maybe you are required to take a 40-hour class and an exam."

"What is it in Mississippi?"

"Well Mark, there are no requirements. It is the only state without a Division of Licensing."

Marks says, "Crazy."

The group continues to make small talk as they have breakfast. The waitress comes over a few times and fills everyone's coffee cups.

Gavin says to their server, "Can you bring me the check, please?"

The woman nods and walks away.

Mark takes the last bite of his pancakes.

Gavin says, "The pancakes must have been good."

Mark laughs and says, "I ordered the normal 6 pancakes. Next time I will order the extra-large stack of 10."

Gavin says, "When the waitress returns change your order from 6 to 10. Take 4 home for later. My client is paying the bill."

"Can I?"

"If the pancakes were that good I would."

The waitress returns with the group's check and hands it over to Gavin.

The private investigator smiles and says, "My friend here wants to change his order from 6 pancakes to 10. He will take the last 4 to go. Here is our ticket."

The waitress smiles and says, "The 4 extra pancakes are on the house. That is the amount you owe."

Gavin says "Thanks" and hands her the law firm's credit card.

The waitress soon returns with a small box and places it on the table along with the credit card and the paid bill. She hands Gavin an ink pen and says, "All I need is your signature and you are all done."

Gavin reviews the charges for the group and signs for 84 dollars. He adds a tip for 16 to make the meal a flat 100. Gavin hands the waitress her pen back along with the signed charge slip and says, "Great service."

Mark picks up his to-go box and the group exits the restaurant. Thy walk over to Mark's mode of transportation and unloads the 2 suitcases. As Mark and Gavin place the luggage into Gavin's rent-a-car's trunk, Sharon says, "Honey, be a good man while I am away. Stay out of trouble."

Mark and Sharon kiss a few times and Mark says, "You do the same while in Gulfport."

Robin rides up front and Sharon is the rear passenger. Robin says as she puts on her seat belt, "Can you put on station 93.3 for me?"

Gavin says, "No problem. What type of music does 93.3 play?"

"Pure country."

Gavin finds the station requested and replies, "Good choice, I like country."

Sharon says, "I hate country."

Gavin says, "We can play 30 minutes of country and 30 minutes of what music you like."

Sharon replies, "No. This trip back to Gulfport is for my sister. I want to make her 100 percent happy. No added stress."

Gavin looks at Robin and says, "The only stress, if any, is when your deposition is taken. Just be 100 percent truthful with your answers and it will be over before you know it. My client, Attorney Morgan, is a nice man. He will prepare you for the deposition. It will be easy. You watch and see."

Robin lets out a deep breath and says, "I do hope you are right."

The 3 fight the traffic to Seattle's airport. Gavin drops the women off at terminal 2 and says, "I will join you in the lobby once I return the rental. Give me 15 minutes."

The women exit the vehicle as a curbside porter approaches them. "Need help with your luggage?"

Sharon says, "Yes. We have 3 pieces of luggage."

Gavin calls the porter over to the driver's window and hands him 20 dollars. He says, "Delta counter please."

The women walk inside the terminal following the porter pushing a cart. Gavin drives away following the signs for rental car returns.

After paying for the rental, Gavin rides the shuttle back to Terminal 2. He joins the women waiting for him. "All done, just need to get our flight tickets."

Gavin and the women wait in the short line. Just 10 minutes later the 3 have their tickets. They board in 1 hour at gate 29.

Gavin says, "Let us go to a coffee shop."

Sharon replies, "I am finished with my 3-cup coffee limit. I will go buy a few magazines."

Gavin hands her a 100-dollar bill. "Here you go, have fun."

Robin says to her sister, "Buy me a People magazine, please."

"Will do. See you in a few minutes."

Robin and Gavin find a quiet corner table in the Coffee Express Shop.

Gavin says, "I love coffee. Ever since I was a police officer on the midnight shift."

Robin says, "I have a cup of coffee in the morning when I first wake up. After that, I have coke or root beer."

Gavin replies, "I will get my coffee and your drink. Save our seats. Do you care for a snack?"

"No."

"I will be right back."

When Gavin returns with the food and drink items, he sees that Sharon has returned. She has a small stack of magazines.

Gavin says to Sharon, "Care for a snack or something to drink?"

"No. I am still full of breakfast."

Gavin sits there quietly while the 2 women look at their magazines.

After 30 minutes Gavin says, "Let us now wait at our gate."

The woman do not say a word but gather their belongings and magazines.

They arrive at their gate but there are few passengers. A Delta employee in uniform says, "Your gate has been changed. It is now gate 7."

The 3 passengers walk down to gate 7 and check in. The ticket agent says, "We will call the first-class section first."

Gavin says to the women, "That is us."

Robin looks at Gavin and says, "You bought us first-class tickets?"

"Yes. Round-trip."

Sharon asks, "Why?"

"Robin is very-important to the law firm. The lawyers need her deposition to settle."

Robin speaks up, "The demand is 20-million, right?"

Gavin says, "Yes."

" How much do you think the settlement will be after my deposition?"

Gavin looks at Robin and replies, "There are about a dozen more people to take depositions of. When all said and done, I think about 12 million at the most."

"I see."

Gavi says, "The law firm needed you in Gulfport. That is why I flew out, to bring you back."

"Just make sure I don't run into Dean or his parents."

Gavin lies and says, "No problem."

The female ticket agent makes an announcement, "Your flight has been changed to gate 16."

The waiting passengers gather their belongings and head to gate 16.

Gavin walks up to the ticket agents and says, "Why are you changing our gate again? This makes our third gate."

An agent replies, "We have a baggage handler strike going on. It has lasted a week now."

Gavin replies, "I hope our luggage reaches our final destination."

The agent says, "We contracted with American Airlines baggage handlers till our local dispute is settled. You can relax, your luggage will get there."

"Gain says, "Good to know."

The 3 soon arrive at gate 16. There is a large crowd in the waiting terminal. Just as the 3 sit down, the announcement comes over the loudspeaker, "Delta will now board first class passengers. Have your tickets and identification ready to show the agents."

Gavin asks the 2 women, "Which one of you wants to be my passenger?"

Robin asks, "You didn't buy 3 seats in a row?"

Gavin says, "The flight was almost full when I bought your sister's ticket. Once I located you in Tacoma and knew I was flying out to escort you, I bought 2 tickets. Once I spoke to your sister and she wanted to come with us I bought the 3rd."

Sharon speaks up, "I will sit with you Gavin. I want to know all about the private investigative business."

Gavin and Sharon sit in seats 7c and b. Robin sits in 2b, in between 2 old ladies.

Seat 7a, the aisle, is for a middle-aged passenger.

Gavin says to Sharon, "You sit by the window."

After all passengers are on board and the door is closed, the Captain makes an announcement. "Hello. This is Captain Young. Our flying time today to Dallas is 4 hours and 10 minutes. Once I level off at 33,000 feet, the stewardesses' will be serving lunch. The weather in Dallas is sunny and 90 degrees."

Sharon says with her eyes closed, "I will take a quick 20-minute nap. Wake me up when lunch arrives, please."

"No problem."

Gavin watches the flight take off down the runway and go air born. He looks at the City of Dallas in the distance as the flight gets higher.

A stewardess pushes a drink cart down the aisle and stops in front of Gavin's row. "Would you like something to drink, sir?"

"A bottle of water, please."

The woman hands Gavin his request and continues down the aisle.

Gavin looks at the woman next to him. She is taking a nap too.

The flight has a small television screen behind each seat. Gavin finds a channel he likes, plugs in a set of head phones and watches the video.

The stewardess comes around with lunch. Gavin wakes Sharon and says, "Lunch is being served."

Sharon with her eyes closed sits up straight and replies, "Smells good."

The stewardess stops in front of Gavin and says, "You have a choice of chicken or beef."

Sharon selects the chicken and Gavin the beef.

"What would you both like to drink?"

Sharon and Gavin both select white wine.

While having lunch Gavin asks, "How long has Robin been in the Tacoma arear?

"A little over 3 weeks."

"What are your sister's plans?"

"Robin plans to go to college and obtain a business degree."

"Why did she divorce Dean?"

"Robin told him many times to quit drinking beer and getting drunk. Dean would stop for a week or 2, but would miss work, get drunk and the cycle would start all over again."

Gavin asks, "Where did Robin and Dean meet?"

"They were high school sweethearts. They dated a long time, then decided one day to get married."

"Why did Dean drink so much?"

"Dean is just like his father. Bill Smith is on his 4th marriage because of his drinking problem."

"Wow! His 4th?"

"Yes, about every 2 years his wife would divorce him. He would just find another woman to move in with and start over."

"Where did Bill Smith meet his women? The internet?"

"No", says Sharon as she takes a sip of wine. In bars."

Gavin asks, "Is Bill still a drinker?"

"Yes and no. His 4th wife, Eva, has him on a tight leash. They have been married now 28 years. He meets with Dean now and then and drinks beer with him. He comes home sober each time."

Gavin replies, "Dean and his father are a tricky pair."

"If Dean didn't drink so much, him and Robin would still be together."

The stewardess stops to collect their food trays. She asks, "Care for another bottle of wine?"

Gavin says, "No thank you."

Once they are alone again Gavin asks, "Why didn't Dean go to AA meetings and kick his drinking habit? His marriage was on the line."

Robin says, "I think Dean went to AA on and off, but the calling for a drink was too strong."

Gavin says, "Too bad Dean is so messed up now and in a wheelchair."

Sharon says, "You are right. I know my sister still cries at night because of his condition."

Gavin is about to ask a question when Robin walks up and says, "Gavin, can you take my aisle seat, 2a, please? Let me sit next to my sister."

"I bought you the 2b seat."

"I know you did. Once we were airborne the women wanted to sit together and talk. I switched to 2a. They talk and talk and loudly, too. I am getting a headache."

Gavin laughs and says, "Sure. The passenger next to me is still sleeping. She does not even snore. She might wake-up when we switch, but if she does, I bet she goes right back to sleep."

Gavin gathers his briefcase and exits his row. Robin climbs over the sleeping passenger and sits next to her sister. "Thank you."

Gavin replies, "No problem." He walks down the aisle to 2a and sits down. The women next to him keep talking.

Gavin closes his eyes and tries to take a nap.

A few hours later the pilot comes on the p.a. system, "Afternoon. This is your pilot. We are 30-minutes from touching down in Dallas. For those of you continuing to Gulfport, Mississippi we will be on the ground about 40-minutes. If you do deboard, bring your boarding pass with you. Thank you for flying Delta."

Gavin was napping when the pilot came on the p.a. system. When he woke, the 2 ladies next to him were still talking. Gavin exits his seat and checks on Sharon and Robin.

Robin asks, "I hope you don't have a headache."

Gavin laughs and replies, "Not yet. Are you 2 getting off or staying on board when we touch-down in Dallas?"

Sharon says, "I will be getting off, but Robin will stay on board."

"Where is the woman in 7a?"

Sharon says, "She just woke up and said she was hungry. She is in the back trying to get something to eat."

The woman returns and says, "Hello." to Gavin.

The private investigator asks, "I am in 2a, care to switch seats with me?"

The woman laughs and says, "No. The 2 women in that row are my mom and her sister. They talk too much."

Gavin says to Sharon and Robin. "I am staying on board as well." Gavin hands Sharon 20-dollars and says, "Can you buy me some assorted snacks?"

"Ok."

The stewardess walks up to Gavin and asks, "Sir, return to your seat please."

"No problem."

The 2 women are still talking when he gets back to 2a. He sits down and asks, "Are you 2 going on to Gulfport, Mississippi?"

One of the women looks at Gavin, and says, "Yes." She turns to her sister and starts talking again.

After the flight lands and Sharon exits the plane, Gavin leaves his seat and takes the empty row seat of 7a. He says to Robin, "The 2 women are still talking. They are going to Gulfport."

Robin laughs and says, "Our luck. Maybe the flight to Gulfport won't be full and we can find an empty row."

Gavin stops a stewardess and asks. "Is the flight full to Gulfport?"

"No."

"Can you find us a row in first class so we 3 can sit together in?

"Stay in row 7. I will redirect anyone that has a seat in row 7 to a different row."

Gavin reaches in his shirt pocket and hands the stewardess his business card. He says, "I will do a free background check or a locate for you and the crew, anywhere in the States."

The woman looks at his busines card and replies, "You are the first private investigator I've met. I will let the crew know. Thanks."

"No problem."

"If a fellow passenger comes to your row, just send him or her to me."

Gavin nods and says, "Thank you, I will."

Robin asks, "Do you like being a private investigator?"

Gavin replies, "No. I love being a private investigator."

"Why?"

"I am my own boss, work my own hours and the pay is pretty good."

Robin asks, "Can I ask how much you make?"

"Sure. I charge 100 dollars an hour and I am terribly busy."

"How did you get the case to find me?"

"I know you don't want to discuss Dean's case so I will skip that part. I was told the law firm client needed to locate you. They needed your deposition as part of a settlement offer. They asked me to find you."

Robin stops the stewardess and says, "Can I have a can of coke?"

"Sure. Be right back."

"How did you find me?"

"I ran data on a data base and discovered you were arrested for shoplifting. I called the jail, and they gave me your bondsman. Your bondsman gave me your sister's number and you know the rest. Tell me about you being arrested for shoplifting?"

"I was stupid. I met a few people and they invited me along to go shopping. I had nothing to do so I went along. I did not shoplift. I knew nothing about them. The police said I was part of a shop lifting ring. They used me as cover while they stole clothes. We were stopped outside the store and arrested. The police had been watching them for weeks. I did a week behind bars. I was innocent the whole time."

Gavin says, "This occurred in Las Vegas, Nevada, Right?"

"Right."

"Why were you in Vegas?"

"I left Gulfport with a man and we were boyfriend and girlfriend, I thought."

"The same man you were with at the party the night you ran into Dean."

Robin says, "Yes."

"Why didn't you stay in Las Vegas?"

"I was being used by the man all along."

Gavin asks, "What do you mean being used?"

"His name is Tony. He had a job offer to be a friend's bartender at a club. Tony had no money, but I did. He used me to fly him out there."

Gavin says, "What happened once you arrived in Las Vegas?"

"Tony went to work, then decided to move into his friend's place. I was just walking the strip checking-out the casino's when the shoplifting group found me."

"You have bad luck choosing the company you are with."

"You are right. That is when I went to Tacoma to be near my sister."

Gavin says, "So when I called, Sharon was screening your calls."

"Yes. Where is my can of coke?"

Gavin says, "I have to use the men's room. I will bring us both back a can of coke."

Gavin leaves their row of seats and enters the restroom. A minute or so later he exits and walks up to a few stewardesses.

"Can I have 2 cans of coke, please?"

One of the women says, "Tell the lady I got stuck with inventory of arriving items and forgot her order." She hands Gavin 2 cans of coke he requested.

"I will tell her. How long till we depart?"

"We will be boarding in 5 minutes." We should be off the ground in 20 minutes."

"Thank you for the cokes and the information."

The stewardess says, "That you for choosing Delta."

Gavin returns to his row and finds Sharon has returned. "Here is the can of coke you requested 10 minutes ago. The stewardess said she got caught-up in inventory of arriving items and just forgot your drink request."

Robin laughs and replies, "My luck."

Gavin asks Sharon, "Want a can of coke?"

"Sure. Thanks."

Gavin hands Sharon the can and says, "No problem."

Sharon hands Gavin a plastic bag with an item inside. "For your office shelf."

Gavin opens the bag and pulls out a miniature building that reads 'Dealey '. He says, "Dealey Plaza Building, A very famous building."

Robin asks, "Why is it famous?"

Gavin looks at her and replies, "This is a famous building but for the wrong reasons."

Robin asks again, "Why?"

Gavin responds, "This is the building from which assassin Harvey Oswald shot and killed President John F. Kennedy on November 22, 1963."

Attached to the gift is a printed tag. Gavin reads aloud, "Visit the 6th floor Museum at Dealey Plaza. The museum is located on the 6th floor of the Dallas County Administration Building overlooking Dealey Plaza. We are in downtown Dallas."

Gavin turns to Sharon and says, "Thank you for thinking of me. I will take you both to my office. We will take some pictures of my new gift sitting on my shelf."

Passengers start arriving from the terminal.

Gavin says, "We have row 7 for us. Let us take our seats so no one else claims them."

Gavin sits in 7a by the aisle. Sharon sits in the middle seat and Robin takes the window, seat 7c. Gavin watches the passenger's board. The stewardess walks down the aisle making sure everyone is buckled-up. The Captain comes over the p.a. system, "Afternoon. This is your Captain. Flying time is 1 hour and 20 minutes to Gulfport, Mississippi. My crew will be around shortly with refreshments and a light snack. Thank you for flying Delta."

Gavin speaks to the 2 women, "My car is in the parking lot at the airport. I will take us straight to our hotel, The Hilton, to check in. My room will be next door to yours. When ready to eat dinner, just knock. I will come over to get you both. What kind of food do you both want?"

Sharon speaks first, "A buffet for me. Robin says, "A good meal. I will eat anything placed in front of me."

Sharon asks, "What do you want for dinner?

Gavin replies, "A buffet sounds good to me. I will take us to The Palace Casino. Their buffet is always good."

Sharon asks, "How far from our hotel is The Palace Casino?"

Gavin replies, "About 13 miles East, just off Highway 90."

Robin leans over and asks, "Tell us a couple of your finished cases."

Gavin laughs and says "There are so many. I was training a new investigator, named Byron and a local case came in. So, we grabbed our cameras to go check the address. We wanted to make sure it was good.

The claimant was an 18-year old white girl involved in an auto accident. She claimed to be totally disabled. The residence was a rural one. When we arrive, we see some man hooking-up a 4-wheeler to a truck. So, we wait down the road to see who is in the truck Abut 10 minutes later the truck departs. It has dark tinted windows. We must follow till we know who the driver is and if there are passengers. The driver stops at a gas station and fills up. The man had to be the father. While I fill up, my new man goes inside with the female passenger. He confirms the woman is our claimant. The insurance company had emailed us her employment file. Byron makes conversation with her while waiting in line. He finds out they are on their way to Mobile, Alabama to drop the 4-wheeler off at a repair shop."

Sharon asks, "How far is Mobile from Gulfport?"

Gavin says, Mobile is 75-miles away. She returns to the truck and they depart. We follow them to a 4-wheeler dealership. They go inside. The claimant, named Noel, is walking fine. She is not wearing any medical devices. I video her inside the dealership which had plenty of display glass."

The stewardess walks down the aisle making sure all the passengers are wearing their seatbelts. She tells Gavin to raise his seat up. The Delta flight then departs for Gulfport.

Gavin continues, "Noel and her dad exit the shop, enter the truck, and depart. They stop at McDonalds drive-up, order a meal and depart. They do not go home. Instead thy drive to Tupelo, Mississippi to a private residence. They unload some luggage from the back of the truck and enter the residence."

Sharon says, "How far to Tupelo from Mobile?"

Gavin answers, "It is 4-hours and 30 minutes."

Robin says, "A long drive.

Gavin says, "It was a long day. I run the home address on data and find out it is her brother's. I depart and fill-up my gas tank. I then go to McDonalds and get us 2 meals. I find a cheap hotel and get a room. I set my alarm for 3 am. I needed to make sure Noel did not depart on me."

The stewardess arrives with a cart full of drinks. "What will you 3 like to have?"

All three asks for cans of coke.

"Care for a bag of potato chips or nuts?"

Sharon wants nuts and the other 2 take barbeque chips.

Gavin asks, "Can I have a second bag of chips, please?"

The stewardess says not a word. She hands Gavin his request then stops at the next row behind them.

Gavin goes on with his story, "They depart at 4:20 am. They drive into some small town called Adams in Tennessee. They park in the parking lot at Bell Witch Cavern."

Sharon laughs at the name and asks, "How far from Tupelo?"

Gavin says, "It was a 4-hour drive. It turns out they were taking a climbing tour with a guide. It started at 9 am. They had a quick bite to eat at the cavern's coffee shop, then joined about 20 other people.

The guide warned, "You must be in good shape to take this tour. We will climb in and out of some tight spaces."

"I went on the tour with a hidden camera to record our claimant."

Sharon asked, "What is a hidden camera?"

Gavin opens his briefcase and pulls out an ink pen.

"This is a hidden camera. The recording lens is hidden behind this little hole."

Gavin points to a hole just above the pen clip. "It has a wide field of view, so you do not have to stand close. When we go to my office, I will show you the video of the claimant."

Robin says, "I can't wait to see the video."

Gavin replies, "We will practice using the pen in my office, then you can visit your mother and video her without her knowing."

Sharon laughs and says, "That will be cool."

Gavin says, "The group climbed into some tight spots. The claimant, named Noel, wrote on a wall, 'Noel was here'. I videoed them exiting the cave all dirty and dusty. They went to the gift shop. My son bought me a ballcap with Bell Witch on it. I have the blue cap on my office shelf. The claimant and her father then drove back to Tupelo and spent the night with her brother. We went the next morning at 4 am to follow her but the truck was already gone."

Robin says, "They left earlier than 4 am?

Gavin relied, "Yes. We thought they would sleep in."

Sharon asks, "What did you 2 do?"

Gavin said, "We ate breakfast, went to The Elvis Presley Museum and drove back to Gulfport. We drove by the claimant's residence and the truck was there. End of case."

Robin asks, "There is an Elvis Museum in Tupelo?"

Gavin replies, "Yes. The man was born in Tupelo."

The stewardess stops by their row and says, "Care for anything else?"

All 3 say no.

The stewardess says, "We will be landing in 15 minutes."

Robin says, "I have to use the powder room."

She leaves her seat and walks to the restroom.

Sharon says, "I bet you have a thousand stories to talk about."

Gavin laughs and says, "True. I do."

Sharon stands up and stretches. "Wil be glad to rest in our hotel room tonight. I should use the powder room as well."

Sharon exits their row and waits for her sister to exit the restroom.

Gavin eats the last of his barbeque chips and grumbles up the bag. He tucks the bag in the seat folder in front of him.

Robin returns to her seat. "Can we have a nice meal as soon as we check-in to our rooms?"

Gavin replies, "Good idea. I am getting hungry as well.

Sharon returns to her seat. Her sister says, "After we check -in to our rooms, we will go eat. I am starved."

Sharon says, "I agree."

The pilot comes on over the p.a. system. "Afternoon folks, this is the Captain. The stewardesses will be walking thru the cabin collecting your trash and making sure your seatbelts are in use. We land in Gulfport in 10 minutes. Thank you for flying with Delta. I hope you will fly Delta again. I will be standing by the pilot's door as you exit."

The flight lands and taxis to their assigned gate. All 3 exit the plane after saying goodbye to the crew. The 3 gather their luggage from baggage and exit the terminal.

They join others for the transportation bus to the long-term parking.

Gavin pulls a ticket out of his wallet and says, "We are parked in row 9, spot 6. I drive a Honda Civic."

The 3 soon arrive at the Honda. Gavin helps the ladies with their luggage and says, "Next stop is the Hilton Hotel in downtown Gulfport."

The 3 make small talk on their 20-minute ride to the Hotel. Gavin grabs a luggage cart and loads all their luggage onto the cart. A bellman pushes the cart into the lobby.

Gavin says, "Wait in the lobby. I will be in shortly. I have to call my client."

Gavin parks his Honda and calls the law firm of Morgan and Rodgers.

Cindy answers on the 4th ring, "Thank you for calling Morgan and Rodgers. How can I help you?"

"Hi Cindy, Gavin here. You are working late."

"Yes. Attorney Morgan is taking an expert witness's deposition. I will maybe leave at 10 pm. Are you back from Tacoma?"

"Yes. I have Attorney Morgan's witness with me. Tell him I will call in the morning. I am tired from the long flight."

Cindy replies, "I will do that."

Gavin says, "I made it to Gig Harbor and bought you a coffee cup and a ballcap for me. Are you working tomorrow as well?"

"No. I have every weekend off."

"Alright, I will see you Monday morning with your gift."

"That was nice of you to do that, Gavin."

"No problem. See you Monday."

They both say goodbye and Gavin enters the hotel. He walks up to the front desk.

"Evening. I have reservations for 2 adjoining rooms. My name is Gavin Parker."

The front desk clerk checks her reservation computer and says, "Yes sir, I have you listed for 2 rooms. Do you need smoking rooms?"

Robin and Sharon hear her and walk up to the front desk.

"We need a non-smoking room with 2 queen beds."

Gavin says, "I need the same thing but connecting please."

Gavin hands the clerk his driver license and credit card.

The clerk takes the items, looks at them and says, "You are a private investigator, correct?"

"Yes. How did you guess?"

"You helped my mom find her brother in Jackson, Mississippi."

"Your mom's name?"

"Bonnie Warren. You didn't even charge her for it either."

"How is your mother doing? Is Jack still with her?"

"My mom is sad. Her brother stayed with her 2 months then went back on the streets doing drugs again."

Gavin hands the clerk his business card. Have her contact me. Tell her I will try again at no charge."

"Really, no charge?"

"Yes. No charge."

"As soon as you leave the front desk, I will call her with the good news. That should cheer her up."

Gavin replies, "Good."

A short while later everyone is in their assigned hotel room. Gavin knocks on their door. The women open the door between rooms and lets Gavin in.

"Soon as you ladies are ready, we will leave for the Palace Casino for the buffet."

Sharon asks, "Why are you not charging the woman to locate her brother?"

She is a receptionist at a large law firm. She makes the lawyers in her office use me for investigations and surveillances. I need to spread the word about me."

Gavin returns to his room and waits.

The women knock 10 minutes later.

Gavin answers, "Come in."

Robin and Sharon walk in and say, "We are starving for a good buffet."

All 3 leave via Gavin's room. It is a quite 15-minute drive to the casino along Highway 90's beach route. The line for the buffet entry is short but the lines at the buffet stations are long. The hostess seats them at a round table for 6 in one of the corners. She says, "Monica will be serving you your drinks."

Gavin says to the ladies, "I will wait for Monica. Go get your meals. What do you want to drink?"

Both want cokes with no ice.

Monica walks over and says, "Evening. My name is Monica. I will be your server." She looks at the slip on the table and says, "What do you 3 want to drink?"

Gavin says, "Coffee for me and the women want coke with no ice."

"I will be right back with your orders."

Gavin calls his mother in Biloxi.

"Hello Mom. Sorry I haven't called for 2 days."

"It has been 4 days, but who is counting, son."

"I had to locate a witness, then fly to Tacoma, Washington and escort the female back to Gulfport. I just arrived an hour ago."

"A witness to what?"

"She was married to a man that was hit by a semi-truck and lived. He is suing for 20 million. He is a quadriplegic. The lawyers will be taking her deposition this week and wanted to make sure she flew to Gulfport. How are you doing with your new boyfriend?"

"Tommy and I are going strong. We booked a week's cruise on Carnival Cruise Line."

"Which port?"

"New Orleans. I forgot the name of the ship."

"When do you depart?"

"Next month."

"I will come by and see you sometime next week."

"Do you want to have dinner with us? I will make meatloaf if you stop by."

"You have a date. Must go now. My witness is walking up to me."

"See you next week. I love you, mom."

"I love you too, son."

Robin returns with a large plate of seafood.

Gavin says, "My turn. I ordered you 2 cokes and a coffee for me. Monica is the server."

Gavin joins a long line waiting at the meat station.

Sharon returns with a large salad and a seafood gumbo soup. She says to her younger sister, "Did you check-out the desserts?"

"I did. I will leave room for sure."

"Me too. That is why I am having a salad."

Robin says, "I can't wait to visit mom."

"Me either," says Sharon taking a bite of her salad.

Monica arrives with their drink orders. Gavin arrives with his plate full of meat.

"Care for anything else?" asks Monica.

Sharon says, "Not at this time, thank you."

Gavin sits down and starts eating his meal.

Sharon says, "Gavin, did you check-out the desserts?

"I sure did. I love the cheesecake and the bread pudding."

The group makes small talk while they have their meal and later their desserts.

Gavin says, "If you 2 want to try your luck at the slot machines I will give you both 2 hundred."

The 3 try their luck at the many different machines. Sharon wins 50 dollars, but Robin and Gavin lose their money.

As they walk to Gavin's car he says, "Did you ladies have fun?"

Sharon replies, "I did. My next vacation will be to Las Vegas."

Robin says, "I did like playing the slot machines. I just hate losing your money."

Gavin laughs and says, "Not my money. My client's money."

They return to their hotel.

Gavin says, "Let us sleep in and have breakfast late. Then we will go buy some nice clothes and get your hair done."

Robin says, "I like that idea."

Once back in his room Gavin makes a list of things he needs to do.

DAY 5 – SATURDAY

Early Saturday morning the hotel's fire alarm goes off. Everyone leaves their rooms and goes outside to the front of the hotel. The fire department shows up and goes inside.

The hotel manager later comes out to his waiting guest and says, "False alarm. Someone on the 5th floor pulled the alarm. You may all return to your rooms."

Gavin turns to the ladies and says, "What a way to wake up."

Robin says, "I am going back to bed."

Sharon replies, "Me too."

Gavin says, "I am up now. Have some calls to make anyway. See you both later. Just knock when you are ready to have breakfast."

Back in his room he calls his friend, Pete, at the library.

"Hi Pete. Did you research the moon the night of my incident.?"

"Yes. No moon. I mailed to your office the moon phase calendar document."

"Thanks Pete. Need any data run?

"Not right now. Have to go, have people at my desk."

Gavin calls the law firm of Morgan and Rodgers.

Cindy answers the telephone, "Good morning, Morgan and Rodgers. How can I direct your call?"

"Hello Cindy. This is Gavin your favorite private investigator."

Cindy laughs and says, "You are the only private investigator I know."

"That is fantastic. Maybe we can have lunch sometime this week and I can tell you all about Gig Harbor."

"I would like that. You need to speak with my boss?"

"Yes. Why are you working on a Saturday?"

"Attorney Morgan asked me to. He is taking many depositions on the Dean Smith case. Let me connect you."

"Attorney Morgan."

"Morning sir. Gavin here."

"Welcome back. How was your trip to Tacoma?"

"It was alright. No problems. I have Robin and her sister in the hotel room next to me."

"Good. Just confirming you will have Robin here in my office tomorrow at 10 am? We are taking her deposition an hour later."

"Yes. I will have her looking pretty for you. I checked the moon the night of the incident and it was a dark moon. I will have the moon phase calendar document in my final report."

"Thank you. Must run. See you and Robin tomorrow."

Gavin flips the channels on his room's television till there is a knock on his interior door.

"Come in."

Robin and Sharon enter, and Robin says, "We are ready for breakfast."

Gavin says, "Good. I was getting hungry." He turns to Robin and says, "Attorney Morgan needs to see you tomorrow at 10 am and your deposition is at 11 am. So, after breakfast we will go buy some new clothes and visit a hair salon."

Robin laughs and replies, "Feels like Christmas, me receiving gifts."

The 3 visit IHOP Restaurant next door.

"Sharon says, "I love pancakes."

After taking their meal and drink orders, Robin asks, "You were once a policeman, right?"

"Eighteen months, mostly on the midnight shift."

Robin asks, "What type of calls were the worse ones?"

"Domestic. The people were already upset and now I was in their home telling them what to do. Some were drunk or high on drugs and some had firearms hidden about their residence."

"Sharon asks, "Is there one domestic call over the others that sticks in your mind?"

"Yes. I hated the calls at the Hunker residence. I was there for the 12th time arresting him for beating his wife. While doing so, the wife was behind me hitting me over the head with a broom handle. She was saying, "Leave him alone I love him.""

Sharon says, "That must have hurt, her hitting you over the head."

"It did. Lucky it was a broom over the head and not a knife in the back."

The waitress brings their pancake orders over with 2 cokes and a coffee.

The 3 make small talk while having breakfast.

Gavin looks at Robin and says, "We will go shopping for new clothes right after breakfast. What store do you want to try first?"

"TJ Maxx. They have my size and style of clothes."

Gavin looks at Sharon and says, "Let us get you a new outfit as well. Just in case the lawyers want to ask you a few questions."

"I like Old Navy."

"Good. Both stores are next to each other at the Crossing Mall."

The group have breakfast and drive over to The Crossing Mall. Gavin says, "Call me when you are about to go to the cashier. I will come over to pay for your items."

Sharon asks, "Where will you be?"

Gavin says, "There is a puzzle store nearby. I will be in there. I love putting puzzles together, besides, they make great birthday gifts."

Robin replies, "I do not have the patients to spend hours putting them together."

Sharon laughs and says, "Me either."

The group split up and go their separate ways.

Robin is the first to call for Gavin.

He walks into TJ Maxx and observes Robin with a few dresses and a pair of white slacks, and a flower designed blouse. He walks up and stands in line with her at the cashier. After paying, they both walk into the Old Navy store. They locate Sharon as she exits a fitting room with a few pair of blue jeans.

After paying for their items they return to Gavin's car. Once inside, Gavin says, "We will go see a friend of mine. She works out of her garage converted into a small hair salon. She will do your hair and facials. All the women I know go to her."

The salon is off a rural road outside Gulfport. There are 4 cars in front of the salon. Gavin escorts the 2 women inside.

A woman in her 40's walks up and says, "Gavin. Long time no see. Give me a hug."

Gavin replies, "Windy, I brought you 2 women from Tacoma, Washington. What ever they want my client will pay. I have their business credit card." Gavin gives the salon owner a big, warm hug. "How is your husband doing?"

"Jack is better. His cancer may be in remission."

"Is he home? Can I walk next door and visit him?"

Windy replies, "No. He is visiting his mother this weekend. I pick him up Monday morning."

"When you do, mention I was asking about him."

"I will. Introduce me to my 2 new customers, please."

Gavin says, "Windy, please meet Robin and her older sister Sharon. Robin is to your left."

Windy looks at Robin and asks, "What would you like me to do today for you?"

Robin replies, "I would like a short, styled haircut."

Windy picks up a booklet from her coffee table in her small waiting room and hands it to Robin. "Here are 40 classy short, hair styles for women. Changing looks and experimenting with styles is a natural thing to do. To look elegant, I recommend combing your looks back, opening your face. Do lighter hair hues and you will easily take years off your face."

Robin says, "I want the Blonde Pixel Cut" and shows Windy the photo from the style book.

Windy says, "A good choice and very popular too."

Sharon looks at her sister's choice and says, "I will have the same haircut."

Windy laughs and says, "That was fast. I wish all my customers were like you 2 ladies."

Gavin says, "I will leave you ladies alone. Windy, call me when you are about finished. I will be at The Moon Creek Mall."

Windy replies, "Will do." She turns to her new customers and asks, "Which one of you wants to go first?"

Robin smiles and says, "I will go first."

Windy hands a television remote to Sharon and says, "You can relax in my office and flip channels."

Sharon takes the remote and replies, "Thanks for the use of your office."

"Glad to be of service."

Windy turns to Robin and says, "First thing I will do is wash your hair. Follow me to the sink."

Robin walks over to the sink and says, "I used to live in Gulfport. My mom lives in Ocean Springs."

Windy washes her new customer's hair, then walks her over to her hair dryer chair.

"Why did you move away to Tacoma?"

"Long story. I followed a man to Las Vegas after my divorce. He was just using me to pay his air fare. Once in Vegas he dumped me. I went to Tacoma to be near my older sister."

Once Robin's hair is dry, Windy walks her over to her hair styling chair.

Windy says, "I have lived in Gulfport all my life. This town is growing. We have 12 casinos and a new aquarium."

Robin replies, "I moved away after my divorce. I wanted a new start."

Windy says, "I have been married 21 years now. How time flies."

Robin asks, "Can I do my own blonde pixel haircuts in the future at home?"

Windy says, "Sure. I will write down all the items you will need. You can purchase the items at your local drug store. It is best if you have someone that can assist you."

Robin yells to her sister in the next room, "Sharon. Come out here and watch me get my haircut. Then in the future we can save money and cut our own hair."

Sharon puts down the television remote and joins her sister.

Windy says, "I will narrate the steps needed as I cut and shape your hair. First, I put a cape on you to protect your clothes. You still will have to wash them afterwards."

Robin says, "Thank you Windy for explain the steps to us."

Windy replies, "I understand. Money is hard to come by for a haircut." Windy starts cutting Robin's long hair into the style she requested. "I use hair clips to separate the back from the front. I cut and trim the back first. The higher you lift the hair, the softer the effect. Then I will blend the front with the back. The last step is using a guarded razor to trim the neck."

Sharon says, "Looks easy enough."

Windy laughs and replies, "It is easy and gets easier over time. Now Sharon just stand back and watch. Robin, no talking, please. Let me focus on giving you an excellent haircut."

Sharon stands back a few feet and Robin says, "Deal. I will be quiet."

Windy says, "I will stop now and then and point out what item I am using. Then when you go to your local drug store you will know what to purchase."

Sharon says, "Thank you."

Windy says, "I washed and dried your hair and placed a cape over your clothes. I am now placing clips to separate the back and front of your hair. Now I am using thinning or texture shears."

About 20-minutes later Windy says, "Now I remove the clips and comb the front of your hair to your back to blend them in. I will now cut the front of the hair."

About 15-minutes later Windy says, "I will now use regular scissors to cut the loose ends."

Sharon stands there taking it all in.

Windy says, "I will use next a wide tooth comb to style the hair."

About 10-minutes later Windy says, "I now will use a guarded razor to trim the neck hairs."

About 5-minutes later Windy removes the cape and says, "You are done. Do you like it?"

Robin looks in the mirror and says, "NO. I love it."

Windy laughs and turns to Sharon. "Now we reverse the roles. Robin will watch and you will be getting the blonde pixel haircut. Let us walk over to the sink to wash your hair. Then we will move over to the hair dryer, then to my hair styling chair and give you a new cape to protect your clothes."

Sharon does as Windy instructs and walks over to the big sink.

Gavin walks into the hair salon. "Ladies I will be sitting in my car when you 2 are ready."

Windy says to both women as she washes Sharon's hair, "Gavin instructed me to give you the deluxe makeover package."

Robin asks? "Which is what?"

Windy walks Sharon over to the hair dryer and says, "I will give you both options when I finish drying Sharon's hair."

Sharon's hair is dry in 20 minutes. Windy walks her over to her hair styling chair and puts a cape over her clothes. "Have a seat, please."

Once in the chair Windy says, "There are 2 types of facials. The first is called Nutri-Facials. It is a nourishing facial and is for dry and dehydrated skin. It consists of a mixture of extracts of algae plants, antioxidants, and moisturizing mask which softens your skin."

Sharon says, "I will go with that one."

Robin asks, "What does the 2nd one do?"

Windy replies, "The Hydra Facial is a treatment that combines extraction and hydration with an infusion of skin rejuvenations anticodons."

Robin says, "I will do the same one my sister is getting."

Windy replies, "Good choice. Do you want to watch me cut your sister's hair or relax in my office and watch television?"

"I'll watch my sister's haircut."

"Fine. Pull up a chair."

Gavin is watching a war movie on his laptop while sitting in his car waiting on the 2 women to finish with their haircuts and facials.

While cutting Sharon's hair, Windy stops now and then to explain the steps to both women what she is doing.

Robin says, "Between my sister and I, and you writing down what tools we will need, we should be able to keep our new hair styles looking professional."

Windy says, "Exactly. With time, you will only get better. Instead of using the word, tools, use the word equipment and hair products."

Sharon looks in the hand-held mirror handed to her by Windy. She looks at her new look and replies, "I look foxy. I should have no problem landing a man, now."

Windy laughs and says, "Which of you want to go first with the facial?"

Sharon says, "Do my sister first. I want to go outside and see what Gavin thinks of my new look."

Windy says, "Fine. I will have your sister come get you when it is your time for the facial."

Windy removes Sharon's cape and motions for Robin to have a seat.

Sharon exits the salon and walks over to Gavin's car and taps on his driver's window. He is busy watching his war movie on his laptop. Sharon knocks on his window again.

Gavin looks up to see Sharon smiling.

He rolls down his driver's window and says, "I say, you look very pretty. Are you all done?"

"No. Our haircuts are done. My sister is having her facial, then I must do mine. Then we will be finished."

Gavin asks, "Are you hungry? Maybe I can order a large pizza and sodas."

"I think that is a good idea, but when the pizza arrives you have to join us."

Gavin says, "Deal. Let the 2 women know, please. I will order a deluxe unless they want different toppings."

Sharon enters the salon and returns to Gavin's side of the car a few minutes later. "A deluxe pizza with cokes will be perfect."

Gavin motions for Sharon to sit on his passenger side. She does. Gavin calls Pizza Hut and places the order. When he hangs up, he says, "The clerk said about 25-minutes. They are just down the road."

Sharon says, "I am hungry."

Gavin replies, "I have been coming to Wendy's salon for a few years now. I always buy us a pizza and soda when she is finished with my hair."

Sharon says, "My haircut is called a blonde pixel cut."

"What type of haircut did your sister get?"

Sharon says, "Robin and I both chose the same haircut. We also choose the same facial. She should be finished in time when the pizza arrives. I don't have to get a facial if there is someplace you need to be."

Gavin says, "Take advantage of my client paying the bill."

"A law firm, right?"

Gavin says, "Yes. Morgan and Rodgers. They need your sister appearing for her deposition and looking professional. This is a 20-million-dollar lawsuit."

"You talk like that amount is nothing. That is a lot of money."

Gavin laughs and says, "It is a lot of money and Dean and his family might receive that amount or even more if this case goes to trial."

"My sister still loves Dean. She gave him so many chances to save their marriage. He would always blow it by coming home drunk."

"Did Dean ever abuse Robin in his drunken stage?"

Sharon replies, "No. Robin told me he would just go to bed and sleep it off. The next day he would bring her flowers and candy and say he would not get drunk again. That cycle of life went on for a few years. Then one day Robin filed for divorce."

Gavin says, "I know he was devastated when Robin told him at the party she filed for divorce. According to Fred, he cried in the bathroom at the party for a long time."

Sharon replies, "I know my sister didn't want to file and then go through the divorce. She was hoping he would stop drinking."

Gavin says, "Between you and I, what did your sister say about meeting Dean at the party and then finding out about his accident?"

Sharon says, "Robin was surprised he showed up. She was glad to be with another male at the party. She wanted someone at the party to mention Robin was seeing someone else. She was hoping this would wake him up to stop drinking. That is why she was surprised he showed up at the party. Robin found out Fred was invited only."

Gavin says, "That makes sense why Dean was surprised to find Robin at the party and upset she was sitting with another man. He had been drinking beer at Fred's house before arriving at the party."

Sharon replies, "Some men never learn. They take us women for granted. What about you Gavin. Do you have a girlfriend?"

"I date now and then but my job keeps me away for many hours a day. No telling when I would arrive home. Take my trip to Tacoma for example. I was surprised I had to go and without notice. Originally I was told just to locate your sister."

Sharon says, "I am hoping my new haircut and facial will attract some men to notice me and ask me out."

Gavin says, "I was dating a nurse for many months, but she finally broke up with me. She left me a note by the kitchen stove. It was 4 days before I found it."

Sharon asks, "What was her name?"

Gavin says, "Sharon."

Sharon laughs and says, "Really?"

"No. It was Donna."

The Pizza Hut delivery vehicle pulls up. A young man exits his vehicle with their order.

Gavin exits his vehicle and says, "I ordered the pizza. Place it on my car hood please. How much do I owe you?"

The Pizza driver hands him his bill and says, "You owe $25.50."

Gavin pulls out his wallet and hands the young man $30.00 dollars and says, "Keep the change."

The driver thanks him and departs. Gavin carries the pizza order into the hair salon.

Gavin says, "Pizza time" and walks over to a round table that seats 4.

Sharon asks, "There are cars in the driveway, where are the customers?"

Gavin laughs and replies, "Windy parks her own cars out front for 2 reasons. One, to make the salon look busy and 2, so she doesn't look alone for safety reasons."

Sharon nods and says, "That is smart."

Gavin says, I told her to do that after my first visit and there were no cars and no other people in her salon. I told her if alone, just close off a door and tell any men that enter for a haircut to please be quite as her husband was in the next room taking a nap. This way, she makes it look like someone is with her."

Sharon says, "I will tell that to a friend of mine that works late in a hair salon."

Gavin replies, "Do. Better to be safe than sorry."

Windy says, "All done with Robin's facial. Let us eat, I am hungry."

The 4 sits around the table and chat, eat pizza and drink their cokes.

Gavin says to Robin, "You look younger girl and pretty, too."

Robin takes a sip of her coke and says, "Thanks."

Windy says to Sharon, "Soon as we finish having pizza, I will do your facial."

Sharon says, "I can't wait. My sister looks relaxed and younger."

Robin replies, "I am relaxed that is for sure."

Gavin laughs and says, "I am always relaxed."

Windy speaks up, "I need to slow down for a few months. I need a small vacation."

After lunch Windy takes Sharon over to her chair to start the facial. Gavin and Robin sit in Henry's vehicle.

Henry says, "I spoke to Attorney Morgan a few hours ago. He needs to meet with you at 10 am tomorrow and your deposition will be an hour later."

"Why so fast?"

Gavin says, "All week the lawyers have been taking depositions in Dean's case. When we arrived in town, I called my client to let him know. The receptionist said Attorney Morgan was in the middle of taking a deposition of an expert."

"An expert in what?"

Gavin says, "I have no clue. Maybe traffic related would be my guess."

Robin replies, "The sooner I get this over with, the more time I will have with my mother."

Gavin says, "Let me drive you and your sister over to your mothers. I will pick you up when it is time to go. Will you 2 need a hotel room in Ocean Springs?"

"No. My mother has rented a 3-bedroom place. She likes to have lots of room. One of her hobbies is oil painting."

"Do you want to call her now and let her know you will be seeing her Monday?"

Robin says, "No. My sister and I want to surprise her. Do you know where Bill Crow's bar is in Biloxi?"

"No clue. Let me look it up on Google."

Gavin looks it up and says, "It is located at 2247 Eisenhower Drive."

"Do you know where Eisenhower Drive is?" asks Robin.

Gavin replies, "Sure do. It is on the same road as the mall."

"We want your help in surprising her we are in town."

"Ok. How?"

"We want to get to the bar about 9:30 am."

Gavin asks, "Does your mom work there?"

"No. That is when she starts drinking and shooting pool."

"Your mom shoots pool at her age?"

"Yes, and she is incredibly good at it too. She drinks almost all day for free from small pool bets with new customers."

Gavin asks, "How will this go do on Monday?"

"You will go in the bar to the woman sitting on the first stool to the right, that is her spot. Ask her to come outside as you need to talk to her about her 2 daughters. Then once outside she will see us standing there."

"Aren't you afraid she may have a heart attack from the shock of seeing her daughters?"

Robin laughs. "She will bring us into the bar for drinks."

Gavin laughs and says, "No problem. Just make sure you don't drink too much beer as your deposition is at 11 am tomorrow."

"I only have 2 beers and after that I drink coke. I was drinking coke at the party when Dean walked in."

Gavin asks, "I think you need to see Dean while you are here. It will do you both good. I have a feeling you still love him."

"I will always love him. We dated for many years starting in high school before we got married a little over 3 years ago. We would still be married if he didn't get drunk almost every night."

Gavin asks, "Want to change subjects?"

"Yes, please."

Gavin says, "After your sister is finished, we will return to the hotel. Order a meal to eat in your room and read or watch television. Tomorrow is the big day. I will leave you at your mother's on Monday till you both are ready to fly back to Tacoma. I will drive you to the airport and give you both 100-dollars for the return trip."

"What are your plans for the next few days? asks Robin.

"I have to do 2 days of surveillance on Dean to document how he is doing and who is taking care of him. I also have to interview the ambulance crew and check the media stations for any evidence they may have on the accident, then I will be finished until the lawyers request something else for me to do."

Robin asks, "Can you put on a country music station for me?"

Gavin laughs and says, "That is a nice way for telling me to shut-up."

Robin replies, "No. I love talking to you. I just wanted to listen to some country music as my sister hates country."

Gavin turns on the radio and a country channel is already dialed in. "See, Robin, I do love country music as well."

"Are you going to take us to your office?"

"Yes. On the way to the airport we will stop in. My office will be on the same road."

"Will you loan us an ink pen camera while we visit our mother?"

Gavin opens his briefcase and hands an ink pen to Robin. "Just hold the top down a few seconds till the blue flashing light is a solid blue. Do the same thing when you want to turn it off. The lens is just below the pen clip and the blue light is right here."

Gavin points to the small hole. "The pen writes as well. Just turn it to the right till the ink pen appears."

Robin practices a few times and says, "Like this?"

Gavin nods his head and replies, "Yes."

Sharon walks out with Windy. Windy motions for Gavin to come to the front porch of her shop. He walks up and Windy says, "2 haircuts are 100 each and 2 facials are 75-dollars each. Total with taxes are 423.40."

Gavin hands her the credit card of the law firm and says, "Make it 150 more for your tip and I will need a receipt."

Gavin returns to his vehicle and Windy enters her shop. Gavin says to Sharon, "The men will be chasing you for sure."

"I sure hope you are right, Gavin."

Windy returns with the receipt to sign, his copy of all charges and the law firm's credit card. Gavin signs and says as he hands Windy her slip, "Nice doing business with you."

Windy bends down and says to the 2 women, "Have a nice flight home. If you need help maintaining the cut, just call me to discuss."

Robin polks her head out the front passenger window and replies, "Thanks, we will."

Gavin toots his horn as they driveaway.

Sharon says, "Can you switch radio stations for me?"

They all agree on a pop radio channel.

Gavin says to Sharon, "We will eat in tonight and go to bed early. I need your sister rested, for her deposition tomorrow."

Sharon replies, "Sure, no problem. I am still jet lagged from our trip from Tacoma to Gulfport anyway. What time do we need to be ready for breakfast?"

Gavin says, "The lawyer's office is 20-minutes away and we have to be there at 10 am, so let us be ready to go downstairs at 8:30 am. We will eat in the hotel restaurant. That gives us an hour to have a meal."

Sharon asks, "What is our plan after my sister's deposition?"

Gavin says, "That is up to you both. I am the taxi. Monday morning is when I will drive you to the bar to meet your mother."

Sharon says, "How do you know about the bar?"

Robin says, "I told Gavin where mother will be while waiting for you to have your facial."

Sharon says, "How about we take in the new Tom Cruise movie."

Robin asks, "Which movie is that?"

Sharon laughs and says, "Mission Impossible 8 or 9. I lost count."

Gavin replies, "I like that idea. Snacks and drinks are on me."

Robin asks, "Snacks are on you or the law firm?"

Gavin laughs and replies, "The law firm."

They go back to their hotel rooms.

Gavin says, "Knock when ready to order. We will charge the meals to our hotel rooms." He closes his interior door and takes a nap.

Attorney Morgan and Attorney Canton discuss settlement.

Attorney Canton says, "In the waiting room are Fred Harris, Officer Sonny Eaton and truck driver Andy Davis. Can we agree to postpone their depositions till early next week?"

Attorney Morgan asks, "Why? Let us at least do one more today."

Attorney Canton says, "My wife just texted me about her brother's birthday party. His gifts are in the trunk of my car."

Attorney Morgan replies, "We can end the whole thing right now if you will accept my settlement offer of 7-million."

Attorney Canton closes his files and reaches for his briefcase on the floor by his feet. "I will come down to 18-million."

Attorney Morgan looks at him and says, "I will offer you 10-million right now to end this."

"I stand at 18-million."

Attorney Morgan closes his files and says, "See you tomorrow at 11am for Robin Smith's deposition."

Attorney Canton says, "Who is your private investigator on my lawsuit?"

Attorney Morgan says, "Gavin Parker of Parker Investigations."

"Never heard of the man. I need to take his deposition as well."

"Let us make him last. He is busy and will need notice."

Attorney Canton stands up and says, "No problem."

Attorney Morgan replies, "Good. I will let the 3 men in the hallway know they are dismissed for now."

"I will tell them. I am leaving the room now."

"So, you won't accept 10-millon? That is a lot of money."

"No. I demand 18-million by Friday next week, or I will go back up to 20-million."

Attorney Morgan says, "See you at 11 am tomorrow."

Attorney Canton says nothing and exits the conference room.

Once in his sports car Attorney Canton calls his client, Bill Smith.

Bill answers on the 3rd ring.

"Hello Bill, Attorney Canton here. Do you have a few minutes?"

"Yes, I do."

"How is Dean doing?"

"Thanks for asking. He is napping."

"I will only be a minute. Attorney Morgan offered us 10 million today while we were taking depositions. I went down to 18 million like we agreed. I told him I will go back up to 20 million if we do not settle at 18-million."

"Well, sir. Eva and I will be happy to accept 10 million."

"I know you will, but your case is worth at least 18 million."

"We trust you, sir. You do what is best for our family."

"Let us see how all the depositions play out. I will know the strength of our case at that time. I might even go up to a 30 million demand."

"Sir, when will you be finished with the depositions?"

"Next week sometime. I will keep you posted."

"Great. Thanks for calling me. When Eva comes home from shopping, I will let her know the latest news."

"Say hello to your wife for me."

"I will."

Both men say their goodbyes.

It is early evening on Saturday when there is a knock on the interior door connecting both hotel rooms.

Gavin says, "Come in."

Robin enters and says, "My sister and I are hungry now."

Gavin turns the television off and walks into their room. "I will have a hamburger, well-done with chips. I want a coke to drink."

Sharon replies, "I want a chicken salad and a coke. I am trying to drop 10 pounds in weight."

Robin replies, "Sharon is always on a diet. I will have what you are having Gavin. I want fries instead of chips if they have them."

Gavin uses their hotel phone to connect with room service. He asks if they have fries. He then places their orders.

Robin hears Gavin order her fries and says, "Thank you for ordering for us."

Gavin laughs and says, "You welcome. Room Service said they will be up here with our orders in about 30-minutes."

Robin asks Gavin, "Can you tell me what I am facing with my deposition tomorrow? I never had one in my life."

"Sure. Tomorrow at 10 am our attorney will go over what questions the other attorney will be asking you regarding your relationship with Dean, why you broke up, where you are living now, if working, basic things like that. Then at 11 am the court reporter will swear you in and you will swear to tell the truth. Try to keep your answers short or to yes, no or I do not know, or I do not remember."

"How long will my deposition be?"

"I think 90-minutes or less. Just take your time, look everyone in the eye and try to relax. I had a few depositions, and they were not bad. Just think of 6 words. Who, what, where, why, when, and how? An example is like, "Where is your cat? What is your cat's name? Why did you name him that name?"

"Who will be in the room with me?"

"Attorneys Morgan and Canton and the court reporter. No one is trying to trip you up. Everyone wants the facts, that is all."

Sharon says, "Robin, it will go smoothly, I just know it."

There is a knock at their hotel door. A man says, "Room Service."

Gavin looks thru the peep hole then opens the door. "Thanks for coming so fast."

"Where do you want me to set the trays down, sir?"

"On the beds will do. How much will you be charging our rooms?"

The man looks at the bill and says 55.40."

Gavin signs the bill and hands the man a 12-dollar tip. "Thanks for coming quickly. We were starving."

"Your welcome sir and thanks for the tip. Enjoy your meals."

Gavin walks the man out and locks the hotel room door.

Gavin clears the small office desk of small things and sits there to enjoy his meal. The women sit on their beds to eat theirs. They make small talk about the weather, the beaches, and the casinos.

Gavin finishes his meal and sets the empty tray outside the women's room. He yawns and says goodnight. He enters his room and closes the door. He is so tired he does not get undressed or pull the covers back. Gavin turns his cell phone off. Within minutes he is asleep.

DAY 6 – SUNDAY

Sunday morning at 7:30 am Gavin's watch alarm goes off. He slowly crawls out of bed and knocks on the women's door.

"Come in" says one of the ladies.

Gavin sticks his head in and says, "Good morning. Today is our big day. Let us go downstairs for breakfast, then go see my attorney a few minutes early. Just knock when ready."

The women nod in agreement and Gavin closes the interior door.

Gavin is getting dressed when his cell phone rings. "Hello?"

"Morning Gavin, I only have a minute. I must cancel Robin's deposition to later in the week, says Attorney Morgan. "I will call you later in the week and we will set a new date."

"No problem, sir. Thanks for calling."

Gavin finishes getting dress and sits on the edge of the bed and turns the television on.

Thirty minutes later there is a knock at Gavin's door. He opens to see two beautiful women dressed in their new outfits. Gavin says, "Change of plans. The deposition will happen later in the week. We are free till then. So, change into something else please and knock again when you are ready for breakfast."

They sit around their Ihop table having pancakes. Gavin asks, "What is your mother's first name?"

Sharon says, "We all call her "Buddy.""

Gavin laughs and says, "Why that name?"

Robin replies, "All her life people have been calling her by Buddy, she wants to be your friend."

"Do you ladies have an address for us to go to this morning to find your mom?"

Robin laughs and says, "She is at The Fill-Me-Up bar in Ocean Springs. We can give you directions as we drive."

"Buddy works there?"

Sharon says, "No. She drinks there till the bar closes. She always sits on the first stool to the right at the counter when you walk in."

Gavin says, "You haven't seen your mom in years, and you know where she will be?"

"Yes," says Sharon.

On the drive to the bar Robin asks, "When we arrive, we want you to bring her outside so we can surprise her we are in town."

Gavin laughs and says, "That should be fun."

Once at the bar Gavin goes in and spots an elderly lady sitting on a stool on the right-side of the bar and walks up to her.

"Are you Buddy?'

"That is my name, who are you?

"My name is Gavin Parker, and I am a private investigator. I need to talk to you about your two daughters. Can we talk outside?"

Buddy stands up and asks, "They are alright, right?"

Gavin smiles and says, "They are doing well in Tacoma, Washington."

Once outside the bar, both women run up saying, "Surprise, Buddy."

All three women stand around hugging and crying.

Gavin waits a few minutes and tells Sharon, "Call me when you want a ride."

Gavin departs in his vehicle and returns to Gulfport.

Sharon and Robin put their arms around their mother and all three enter the busy bar.

Bill Smith receives a telephone call from their attorney, Joe Canton.

"Morning Bill, this is Joe Canton. Is this a good time to talk about your case?"

"Yes sir."

"I hired another expert, and he says to demand thirty million and try to settle for twenty million."

"Well sir, we could use any money right now for our son, Dean."

"I was going to ask how Dean is doing today?"

"Dean sleeps a lot, which is good. He needs his rest."

"I have to go back to my depositions. I will call you when I can."

"Thanks, sir, for calling."

Gavin gives Cindy a call.

"Good Morning, Morgan and Rodgers Law Firm" says Cindy when she answers.

"Hi, stranger. How has life been treating you?" asks Gavin.

"I am doing good; I was wondering when you would be calling me."

"I have been busy with the two women from Tacoma, taking them everywhere, feeding them, I feel like a babysitter sometimes."

Cindy laughs and replies, "I bet you don't mind hanging around two women all day. I bet they are pretty as well."

"They are pretty. I am free till they want a ride back to the hotel. They are with their mother in Ocean Springs".

Cindy says, "It is crazy here in our office with all the depositions going on with the young man that was struck by the semi."

"Attorney Morgan called me the other day and changed my witness's deposition till Wednesday."

Cindy says, "Between you and me Gavin, they are trying to settle."

"Well I hope they do. This case has been a lot of work, flying to Tacoma, escorting two women 24-7 and neglecting my other cases. Therefore, I am in my office now. To try to get caught-up."

"Don't forget the trip to Gig Harbor and my gifts."

Gavin laughs and says, "I must focus on work now, you have a super day Cindy."

Cindy laughs and says, "You too."

Gavin plays back his answering machine for any messages.

In between depositions, Attorneys Morgan and Canton go back and forth on the settlement attempt on Dean Smith's case.

Attorney Canton says, "Our demand now is thirty million. I hired a financial expert, and he says that is what we should ask for and then settle for twenty million."

Attorney Morgan replies, "Thirty is out for sure. I would just go to trial and see what the jury would say."

"Add in my client everyday in court in a wheelchair and the jury may issue more than thirty million."

"I am aware of that factor. It is a risk my client is willing to take."

"It is time to take the deposition of your driver, Andy Davis. Let us discuss the settlement after Mr. Davis's deposition."

Both men enter the court reporter's room and say hello to Mr. Davis.

Attorney Morgan turns to the court report, a female and says, "Swear the witness in please."

Attorney Canton gets the driver to admit he has a bad habit of texting and driving but claims he was not on his cell phone at the time of the accident.

Attorney Morgan asks the driver, "Did you cross the line in the road with your semi and strike the victim, Dean Smith?"

"No sir I did not. He suddenly without warning just jumped in front of me."

"How long have you been driving big rigs?"

"I am on my thirty-sixth year."

Attorney Morgan asks, "How many tickets and accidents have you had during this time?"

"My record is clean, and I have traveled to all 50 states too. I love to drive."

"You have been to Alaska and Hawaii as a truck driver?" asks Attorney Morgan.

"Yes sir. I have worked for six different truck companies in my lifetime."

Attorney Morgan asks, were you ever fired from an employer?"

"No sir, the pay was low, so I moved on."

The deposition lasted about thirty minutes more.

While waiting to take the deposition of the next witness, the tow truck driver, the attorneys returned to discussing a fair settlement.

Attorney Canton says with a grin, "No jury will think my client just stepped in front of a moving semi-truck traveling 25 miles and hour down the roadway. Then the jury will see my client in a wheelchair every day of the trial. I will present medical experts that will tell the jury what care for life my client will need. So, I am sure if I ask for thirty million dollars the jury will maybe reward my client even more. So, my demand now is twenty-five million."

Attorney Morgan shakes his head from side-to-side and replies, "No doubt you have a strong case, and you may be right about the jury rewarding you a lot of money. My client knows this too, so, they came up to fifteen million. Check with your client and get back to me when you can."

Attorney Canton says, "Our next deposition is of one of the ambulance crew at the accident scene. I will speak to my client when the deposition is finished."

It is late in the afternoon when Sharon gives Gavin a call.

Sharon says, "Gavin are you busy, can you talk right now?"

Gavin replies, "No I can talk, what is up, are you ready for me to pick you two up?"

"No. My sister and mother are slowly getting drunk. The bar offers a free buffet, then after that closes, a county western band will come on. So, we will be here late into the night."

"What about you Sharon, are you slowly getting drunk too?"

Sharon laughs and replies, "That is hard to do if you are drinking soda only.

"No matter the hour just call my cell when you three are ready to go home."

Sharon says, "I will give you a twenty-minute heads up when we are ready."

Gavin says, "Thanks. Have fun with your mother and thanks too for calling."

After the deposition Attorney Canton made a phone call to Bill and Eva Smith.

"Hello" said Eva on the fourth ring.

"hello Eva, this is Attorney Canton. I do not have much time to talk. I am in the middle of taking depositions. Is Bill there as well?"

"He is in the garage, let me call him".

A minute later Bill picks up the telephone and says "Hello."

Attorney Canton says, "I have a settlement offer of fifteen million. I need an answer if you will take that low amount?"

Bill replies, "In your last call you mentioned thirty million."

Attorney Canton says, "The closer we get to trial the offers will get higher as the insurance company does not want to risk a huge award."

Bill asks, "What do you think we should do? Fifteen million is a lot to turn down."

Attorney Canton says, "True Bill, but I am sure if we hold out till just before trial the offer will go up."

Bill replies, "We turn the fifteen million dollars offer down."

"One more thing, how is your son doing today?"

Dean is doing good today; he is in the living room watching television."

Good to hear. I must return to my depositions. I will call you with any other news."

Attorney Canton approaches Attorney Morgan and says, "I spoke to my clients just now and we will turn down your latest offer."

"What! Fifteen Million Dollars you guys turned down; I don't believe it."

Attorney Canton replies, "Believe it."

Attorney Morgan says, "There is a chance the jury will believe my driver that your client stepped in front of his truck. Your client was crying earlier that night after finding out from his wife that she filed for divorce."

Attorney Canton laughs and says, "The jury will not believe for one second that he would step in front of a moving semi-truck. Who does that anyway?"

Attorney Morgan replies, "A depressed man knowing his wife was going to divorce him."

Attorney Canton says, "If that is what you believe, then we will see you in court and we will let the wise jury decide."

Both lawyers enter the deposition room for the next witness on their list.

Gavin calls the Morgan and Rodgers Law Office. A different woman answers the telephone.

"Hello, this is Gavin Parker, can I speak with Attorney Morgan's secretary please."

"Yes sir, I will connect you now."

"Barbara speaking."

"Hello Barbara, this is Gavin Parker."

"How can I assist you, Gavin?"

"I was wondering why all the depositions on the Dean Smith case all of a sudden."

"My boss has another trial after this one and he wanted to speed things up. He is also hoping to settle the case. He is worried what a jury would do."

"Any settlement offers?"

"Yes. The insurance company offered fifteen million dollars and the plaintiff turned it down."

Gavin gasps and says, "Wow."

Barbara asks, "Is there anything I can do for you young man?"

"No. I am just killing time till my witness contacts me for a ride. She is visiting her mother in Ocean Springs."

"I will tell my boss you called. I have to go back to work."

Gavin says goodbye and hangs up.

Sharon calls at eleven pm.

"Can you come get us. They are fully wasted, and I am tired and want to go to bed."

"I will be there in twenty minutes. I am leaving now as we speak."

Gavin enters his vehicle and heads East on Highway 90 for Ocean Springs. In the daytime it is a beautiful drive. The waves crashing to shore from the Gulf of Mexico are a pretty sight to see when waiting at a red light.

Gavin arrives at the bar. Waiting out front is Sharon.

"Help me bring my sister and my mother out of the bar. They are still drinking."

Gavin and Sharon enter the crowded bar and find Robin and their mother at the bar. They have drinks in their hands. Gavin says, "Alright ladies. It is time for your ride home."

Robin replies, "Do I have to leave?"

Gavin lies and says, "Attorney Morgan says your deposition is at 4 pm tomorrow. You have to be sober by then."

Gavin helps the women to his car. Robin sits in the front passenger side and the other two sits in the back.

Gavin asks, "Where does your mom live?"

Sharon replies, "Just drive and I will direct you to her house. It is on Miller Drive, about four miles away."

During the drive Robin says, "Dean wrote me a letter a couple of weeks prior to his accident. He said if I divorced him, he did not want to live. Maybe I should cancel the divorce proceedings and give him one more chance. I do love him with all my heart." Robin starts to cry.

Gavin asks, "Do you really love him Robin or is it the liquor talking?"

"No, I do love him. I want to go see him after I drop my mother off."

Gavin says, "I will take you to see your husband after your deposition is taken."

"Robin replies, "You have a deal."

Gavin asks, "Do you still have that letter?"

Robin replies, "I never throw anything away. It must be in a box in the garage. I went out West and had to leave all I own in my mother's garage.

Robin keeps talking with a slurred speech.

Gavin arrives at the house on Miller Drive.

Sharon opens the garage with a remote.

Gavin asks, "Where did you get the remote?"

While helping her mother into the house, Sharon replies, "I retrieved it from my mother's car at the bar."

Robin locates her mother's bed and crawls inside the covers. Sharon helps her mother into the same bed and covers her up.

Sharon turns out the bedroom light and closes the door. Sharon walks to the living room couch and lays down. Sharon asks for a blanket from the hall closet. Gavin retrieves the blanket and gives it to Sharon.

"Thank you, Gavin." Sharon turns over and falls asleep.

Gavin enters the garage and turns on the light. There are at least twenty-five boxes stacked on one side of the two-car garage. Gavin opens the first box and starts looking for the letter Dean wrote his wife.

Gavin knows the letter Dean wrote is especially important to find. The letter will show Dean's state of mind the night of the accident. The letter may convince a jury that Dean stepped in front of the semi-truck to die on purpose. This is because Dean's wife told him only hours before at the party she filed for divorce.

No letter was in box number one. Gavin opened the next box. Inside were many papers to read. Gavin kept opening the boxes in the garage. About four hours later Gavin located the letter.

"Robin my love, I do not want a divorce. I promise to stop drinking. I have promised many times before to stop drinking, but I mean it this time. If you ever file for a divorce, I do not want to live. You are my whole life. I love you with all my heart. Give me another chance. I will show you the man I was when we first married. I love you. Love Dean."

The letter is dated and signed exactly 8-days prior to Dean's accident.

Gavin folds the letter up and places it in his back pocket. Gavin restacks all the boxes and turns out the garage light. Gavin walks to his car, reclines the front eat and tries to fall asleep.

At eleven-thirty am there is a loud tap on the driver's window of Gavin's car. Gavin rolls down his window and says, "Hello, Buddy."

"Morning. Come inside, I have coffee and toast ready."

"Are your daughters up yet?

"Yes. Robin is in the shower and Sharon is sitting at the breakfast table."

At breakfast Gavin lies to Robin.

"I searched your boxes in the garage for hours but did not find the letter you mentioned last night on the way home from the bar."

Robin gives Gavin a puzzled look and replies, "What letter are we talking about?"

Gavin says, "The letter that your husband wrote a week or two ago where he states he does not want to live if you two get divorced."

Robin says, "Dean did write it and it has to be in one of the boxes. Us three will search for the letter right after breakfast. What time is my deposition?"

"hanks for reminding me. The lawyer called and said your deposition will be in a few days."

"Great news," replies Robin. "We can stay a few more days with our mother."

Gavin laughs and says, "No more drinking in the bar till your deposition is over."

The four sits around the breakfast table and tell stories.

Attorney Morgan is in the deposition room when Attorney Canton walks in with his briefcase.

Attorney Morgan asks, "Do you care for a cup of coffee?"

Attorney Canton replies, "No thanks. I drank a few cups on the way over here."

Attorney Morgan says, "It is not too late to take our settlement offer of fifteen million dollars."

Attorney Canton looks over at the attorney and replies, "No thanks. We will just go to trial and let the jury determine our amount."

Attorney Morgan says, "We may win a direct verdict and if we do your client ends up with zero money. Did you warn them about that?"

Attorney Canton sits down at the long conference table and opens up his briefcase and says, "My client knows the risk but they are very confident in my skills to settle their case or go to trial and obtain a verdict."

The court reporter walks in with her equipment and says, "Morning gentlemen."

Both answers, "Good morning to you."

The court reporter asks, "Can I have the name of the first person we are taking the deposition of this morning."

Attorney Morgan replies, "Mr. Chuck Press, the owner of Silver Streak Freight Forwarders."

Attorney Morgan turns to Attorney Canton and says, "His best driver claimed from day one that your client stepped in front of him for no reason."

Attorney Canton laughs and replies, "My witness, Fred Harris claims that Dean was checking his mailbox by the edge of the highway when your client crossed the line and struck his friend."

Cindy knocks on the conference door and enters with Mr. Chuck Press." Gentlemen, your nine am witness is here, Mr. Chuck Press."

Attorney Morgan stands up, shakes the man's hand and says, "Thank you for coming this morning. Please sit to my left."

Attorney Canton says to the witness, "My name is Attorney Canton, and my client is the victim in this case, a young man named Dean Smith."

Attorney Morgan turns to the court report and says, "Please swear the witness in."

Gavin says good-bye to the three ladies, enters his car and departs the area. Once in his car, he calls the law firm of Morgan and Rodgers. Cindy answers the telephone.

"Good morning, you have reached the law firm of Morgan and Rodgers, how can I assist you today?"

"Hi Cindy, you sound cheerful today."

Cindy laughs and replies, "Morning Gavin. I am always cheerful."

Gavin asks for Attorney Morgan.

Cindy replies, "My boss is in depositions all day."

Gavin says, Please, tell him I need to meet him in person today. Tell him I uncovered evidence in the Dean Smith case he needs to know about."

"Can you tell me what evidence you uncovered?"

Gavin laughs and says, "Nope. I will tell you when I see you in person. How about lunch at Taco Bell?"

"I have lunch from one to two pm today."

Gavin replies, "Great. The Taco Bell on 8th street. Do you want me to pick you up?"

Cindy says, "No. I need to walk and stretch my legs as I sit all day."

Gavin laughs and says, "I will see you at one then, bye."

At one pm Gavin enters Taco bell and joins Cindy at a corner table.

"How was your walk over to Taco Bell?"

"Great. Only problem is the constructions workers that whistle at me when I walk by."

Gavin says, "I get the same thing. I hate it."

Cindy laughs.

Gavin pulls out the letter that Dean wrote to Robin.

"Do you know anything about the Dean Smith case?"

Cindy says, "Only that a young man was struck by a semi-truck and almost died."

Gavin replies, "The semi-truck driver claimed the man just stepped in front of him without warning. The witness for the victim claims the driver crossed the line and struck the victim as he checked his mailbox, which was located at the edge of the road."

Cindy looks at Gavin and says, "So, who is telling the truth?"

Gavin replies, "The driver received a ticket for careless driving, so I think a jury would claim it was the driver's fault, besides who steps in front of a semi-truck?"

"Not me," Cindy says.

"He wrote his wife a letter just 8 days prior to the semi-truck accident. She said she was going to file for divorce. I found the letter in my witnesses' house. Now on the night of the accident he met her at a party. She told him she just filed for divorce and gave him her wedding ring back to him. So, he is depressed and stepped in front of the semi. That is what this letter tells me. Here read it."

Gavin hands Cindy the letter.

A few minutes later Cindy says, "This is an important letter for sure. It shows his state of mind."

Gavin replies, "More important it is dated and signed by Dean Smith."

Cindy says, "I am hungry let us have lunch."

"What do you want?"

Cindy says, "The soft taco special with a coke."

Gavin says, "I will have the same thing and will be right back."

Five minutes later Gavin returns with two boxes that look like lunch boxes ad says, "Here you go."

Gavin and Cindy make small talk as they have their lunch. When they are finished with their lunch, Cindy stands up.

"I have to get back to work."

"I will walk you back. The construction workers should not whistle if they see a man with you."

"Thanks. I would like protection."

Gavin walks Cindy the 9 blocks to her office. The construction crew still whistled and shouted at her."

"See, how they don't care if a man is with me."

Gavin says, "Make sure attorney Morgan calls me but don't mention I found a letter."

Cindy says, "Will do. Thanks for lunch."

"You welcome. Let us do it again sometime."

"Ok. Bye."

Gavin walks back to his car located at Taco Bell, but he makes one stop on the way.

At the construction site he asks for the foreman.

An older man walks up and says, "I am the Foreman. My name is Steve Wilson."

Gavin says, your men are whistling at all the women that walk by, including my sister. This has to stop."

"I cannot make my men stop whistling at the women walking by."

Gavin replies, "I can. I will have forty women with signs start picketing this site."

"Steve shakes his head and says, "The whistling will stop."

Gavin shakes his hand and replies, "Thank you sir."

Gavin calls Cindy and says, "The whistling will stop."

"How sure are you it will stop?"

"I told them all my brother is Superman and he will kick all their butts if they whistle again."

Cindy just laughs and says, "You are to funny."

Gavin replies, "Next time you go by and they whistle, just let me know."

"Will do. Attorney Morgan is taking a deposition, but I will make sure he calls you."

"Thanks," Cindy." Bye."

Gavin is driving to his office when Sharon calls him.

"Hello?" says Gavin while waiting at a traffic light.

"Sharon here, how are you doing?"

"I just had lunch with a woman I am crazy about."

"Good for you, glad to hear it."

Gavin asks, "What about you and your sister, how are you both doing?"

"We are tired from looking into my sister's boxes in the garage for that letter you told us about."

Gavin says, "Maybe it was thrown away after Robin read it. She received it months ago."

Sharon replies, "We have six more boxes to go."

Gavin pulls up to the building his office is at and says, "I wish you all good luck in your search. When do you want me to pick you both up?"

"How about eight am before my mother returns to the bar."

"See you both then and thanks for calling Sharon."

Sharon and Gavin both say good-bye to each other.

An hour later Gavin receives the call he has been waiting for.

"This is Attorney Morgan, what do you need Gavin?"

"Sir, I need to see you in person. I found evidence that may win you the case against Attorney Canton."

"What kind of evidence are you talking about?"

"A letter written, signed and dated by Dean Smith to his wife, Robin that Dean wrote eight days before his accident. He tells Robin that if she divorces him, he does not want to live. Then at the party remember, the night of the accident, she tells him she filed for divorce and returned her wedding ring. So, this means he was depressed and stepped in front of the semi just like your client claimed from day one."

"Where is this letter right now?"

"In my back pocket."

"Bring this important letter to my office at five pm today for me to read."

"Yes sir. See you at five."

Both men hang up after saying goodbye.

At 4:40 pm Gavin drives off to Morgan & Rodgers Law firm. Barbara, Attorney Morgan's secretary is sitting at the reception desk.

Gavin asks, "Where is Cindy?"

"She had to go home early. She had food poisoning from having lunch at Taco Bell."

"Wow really?

"Let me escort you to the conference room."

Once inside the conference room Barbara asks, "Care for something to drink?"

"No Thanks."

A few minutes later both law partners enter the conference room.

Attorney Morgan asks, "Well Gavin let us see what you have found."

Gavin pulls the letter from his back pocket and hands it over.

Gavin says, "This letter proves Dean Smith's state of mind regarding getting a divorce. Remember, the night of the party Dean ran into his wife. She told him she just filed for divorce. Robin even returned her wedding ring over to him. So, Dean knew that night his relationship with Robin was over. I believe he stepped in front of the semi-truck on purpose just like your client said from day one."

Attorney Morgan reads the letter and then hands it to his partner to read. Attorney Morgan picks up the telephone and dials an extension then says, "Barbara please come in the conference room."

A few minutes later Barbara does. Attorney Rodgers returns the letter to his partner.

Attorney Morgan hands the letter to Barbara and says, "Please make me fie copies."

Barbara exits the room with the letter in her hand.

Attorney Morgan turns to Gavin and says, "This letter is especially important. It does show Dean Smith's state of mind. If we go all the way to court, I believe the jury will find in our favor. It will show our truck driver was telling the truth from day one."

Attorney Rodgers says, "I will now call Attorney Canton and ask him to return to our office for settlement talks." Attorney Rodgers then leaves the room.

Attorney Morgan turns to Gavin and asks, "Tell me how you came across this letter."

Gavin says, "I was driving Robin to her mother's house when she mentioned the letter. Once at the house I had to search about forth boxes located in the garage. Lucky for us Robin throws nothing away."

Attorney Morgan says, "Lucky for us as well, Dean signed and dated the letter."

Attorney Rodgers returns to the conference room and says, "Attorney Canton said he will be here at ten am tomorrow."

Attorney Morgan turns to Gavin and says, "At ten am tomorrow I want you to speak with Fred Harris and show him a copy of the letter. Obtain the truth out of him on what happened the night the semi-trailer struck his friend.

"Yes sir."

Gavin returns to his office and prepares the questions he plans to ask Fred Harris. While making the list of questions his office phone rings. Gavin is surprised he is receiving a call so late.

"Good Evening, Parker Investigations."

Cindy says, "How did the meeting go with my boss?"

"First of all, how are you doing? Barbara told me you had food poisoning."

"I had to lie. I needed time off to go shopping for a birthday present for my mother."

"That is good news that you are fine. I felt bad all day as I invited you to Taco Bell for lunch."

"I have been so busy at work that I almost forgot my mother's birthday."

"How old is your mother and when is her birthday?"

"Yesterday was her fifty-seventh birthday. I realized it at three pm. We were to meet at six pm for dinner at Billy's Seafood Restaurant on fourth avenue."

Gavin laughs and says, "I did that once with my mother too. I felt so bad. Work will do that, make you forget."

"So, how was your meeting?"

"Good. I must meet with the witness, Fred Harris, at ten am. He told everyone in his deposition that Fred Smith was checking his mailbox by the side of the road when he was struck by the semi-truck. As you know, the letter I found proves his emotional state. The divorce warning, then Robin telling him at the party she filed for divorce was too much for him. I just have to get the truth out of him."

"Why ten am tomorrow?"

"Attorney Morgan is meeting with Attorney Canton at ten am in the conference room. He wants to make sure Fred Harris doesn't have a chance to tell him about the letter."

"Please call me when you are finished meeting with Fred Harris. I will be at home."

"You are not going to work?"

Cindy laughs and says, "No. I am sick remember."

"I will call your cell phone once I am back in my car."

Cindy and Gavin talk for twenty-minutes more before calling it a night."

James Paul Ellison

DAY 7 – MONDAY

Gavin knocks on Fred Harris's door at ten am sharp. Fred comes to the door and says, "Hello."

Gavin shakes the young man's hand and asks, "Can you join me in my car?"

Fred has a puzzled look on his face and asks, "Why?"

Gavin replies, "Dean Smith's lawyer is in settlement discussions with my boss, Attorney Morgan, and some questions came up regarding the accident."

Fred closes the front door behind him and walks over to Gavin's car and sits in the passenger side.

Gavin says, "Do you know what the word deception means?"

"It means falsehood."

Gavin looks at Fred and says, "It means deceiving someone."

"So why are you telling me this?"

"Fred, I need the truth of what happened the night of your friend's accident."

"I told the police the truth. Dean was checking his mailbox when the semi-truck crossed the line and hit my friend."

Gavin pulls out the letter from his back pocket and hands the letter over to Fred and says, "I discovered this letter yesterday at Robin's mother house. Please read it."

Fred reads the letter and hands it back to Gavin.

Gavin says," Did you noticed the letter is dated and signed by your friend just eight days prior to the semi-truck accident?"

"Yes."

Gavin says, "Dean met Robin at the party and was told she filed for divorce. Robin even returned her wedding ring to him. Your friend was so depressed that a few hours later he stepped in front of the semi-truck to kill himself."

Fred starts to speak but is cutoff by Gavin.

"Fred, the letter shows your friend's state of mind. He says in the letter "If we get divorced, I do not want to live." So, tell me the truth. You can be arrested by the police for making a false statement."

Fred looks at Gavin and nods his head.

Gavin turns his tape recorder on.

"This is Gavin Parker, a private investigator with Parker Investigations. Today's date is March seventh in the year 2021. I am meeting with Fred Harris in my car in front of his house. This is involving his friend Dean Smith being struck by a semi- truck three months ago. Do I have your permission to tape record you today?"

"Yes, you do."

"Are you aware I am tape recording you?"

"" Yes, I do."

"Fred, in your own words can you tell me please what occurred the night of the accident?"

"Dean and I went to a party and ran into his wife Robin who also attended the same party. He was incredibly happy to see her. They had been separated for a few weeks. Robin told him she just filed for divorce and handed him back her wedding ring. Dean went into the restroom and started crying. He was very depressed. He went back into the party and started drinking beers. Robin left the party with an unknown man at one am. We left the party at two am. I drove Dean home. I pulled up in his driveway to escort him to his front door, when suddenly my friend said, "I will show her" and he ran into the road and stepped in front of the semi-truck."

Gavin interrupts and says, "How dark was it that night?"

"Very dark as Dean lived on a rural highway with no streetlights."

Gavin asks, "So, why did you give the police a false statement that night?"

"Because Mr. Smith asked me to. He said the family did not have any medical coverage and by suing the trunk company, Dean would be taken care of."

Gavin shakes his head and replies, "The truck driver, Andy Davis, claimed from the beginning that Dean suddenly stepped in front of him without warning."

Fed starts to cry and says, "The driver was telling the truth. I am sorry I made a false statement. I did not want to deceive anyone. Mt Smith asked me to lie, besides, I wanted to help my friend."

Gavin says, "Fred, did I have your permission to tape record you today?"

"Yes."

"This ends the statement of Fred Harris." Gavin turns the tape recorder off.

Fred asks, "Will I get into any trouble for my deception?"

"No, because you told the truth today. Now go inside your house and call no one. I will call you later today."

Both men shake hands. Fred exits Gavin's car and enters his home.

Gavin calls the law firm and speaks to Attorney Morgan who was waiting for his call.

"Well Gavin, "Were you able to speak with Fred Harris?"

"Yes sir. Fred was told to lie about the truck driver crossing the line and striking Dean Smith. He was told to lie by Mr. Smith as the family had no medical insurance."

Attorney Morgan asks, "Do you have the confession on tape?"

"Yes, I do."

"Please come to my law practice now with the tape confession."

"Are you in negotiations with Attorney Canton?"

"Yes. I stepped away just to take your call."

Gavin replies, "I will be in your office in twenty minutes."

Both men say their goodbyes.

Attorney Morgan returns to the conference room. "Sorry, I had to take that call, Joe."

"No problem, Henry. Why did you take back your last offer of fifteen million dollars?"

"Because I have discovered new evidence that will show that your client stepped in front of the semi-truck on purpose."

Attorney Joe Canton looks surprised at the news.

"What evidence is that?"

"I will gladly show you once my private investigator arrives in about twenty minutes."

Barbara walks in with two cups of hot coffee on a tray, along with cream and sugar.

"I made a fresh pot."

Both attorneys reach for their hot cups of coffee after saying thank you.

Gavin calls Cindy while driving to the law firm.

"I have Fred Harris's statement on tape. He finally told me the truth. Dean's dad asked him to lie for him as the family had no medical coverage. I am driving to Attorney Morgan's office now. He is in a conference with Attorney Joe Canton."

"I wish I could be there to see all the fireworks going off in that room," says Cindy.

Gavin replies, "Attorney Canton demanded at one time for thirty million dollars. He will have to lower his demand for sure once he sees and hears the new evidence."

Cindy replies, "My boss will give you a big bonus if this works out."

Gavin replies, "I will feel sad for the family if they receive no money. If this case goes to trial, I see no jury giving the family any money. The plaintiff stepped in front of the semi-truck on purpose."

Cindy says, "I never thought of that."

Gavin says, "I am pulling up to the law firm's office now. Wish us luck in the negotiations."

"My fingers and toes are crossed," says Cindy with a laugh.

Gavin walks into the law office. Barbara is at the reception desk waiting on him.

"I am to take you straight to the conference room. Would you like something to drink?"

"Yes, I would. A bottle of water."

Barbara knocks on the conference door before entering with Gavin. Barbara says, "Here is private investigator Gavin Parker of Parker Investigations."

Both attorneys stand up and shake his hand.

Attorney Morgan pulls out a chair and motions for Gavin to have a seat.

Attorney Canton asks, "What evidence do you have against my client?"

Attorney Morgan opens his file on the case and hands Attorney Canton the letter Dean wrote to his wife, Robin.

Attorney Canton reads the letter and says, "My client says he does not want to live and wrote this letter eight day prior to his accident. He was depressed when he wrote it. This letter has nothing to do with his accident. Your client crossed the line and struck my client while he was checking his mailbox."

Attorney Morgan turns to Gavin and says, "Play the confession of Fred Harris from this morning."

Gavin pulls out his tape recorder. Before playing the tape, Gavin says, "I met with Fred Harris at his house this morning. I showed him the letter that Dean wrote and said to Fred, "You committed deception by claiming the semi-truck driver struck your friend."

Attorney Canton asks, "What else is on the recorded tape?"

Gavin turns on the tape recorder for all to listen.

After the tape is finished, Attorney Morgan turns to Attorney Canton and says, "Your client also committed deception by having Fred Harris lie about my client crossing the road, when in fact your client jumped in front of the semi-truck on purpose."

Attorney Canton says, "Let me step out of the room and give my client a call."

"Go ahead,"" says Attorney Morgan as he takes the tape recorder from Gavin.

Once alone, Attorney Morgan turns to Gavin and says, "Great job. You just saved my client from paying out millions of dollars."

Attorney Canton calls Bill Smith at home.

Bill answers and say's "The Smith Residence."

"Morning Bill, Joe Canton speaking. We have a serious problem."

"What problem is that Sir?

"You told Fred Harris to lie."

"Lie about what sir?"

"To lie by telling the police the truck driver crossed the line and struck your son, when in fact your son jumped in front of the semi-truck on purpose."

"Who told you that bullshit story?"

"Fred Harris did this morning in a taped confession to a private investigator. I just heard the tape. Fred claims you told him to lie because you have no medical coverage."

There is no sound for about thirty seconds. Bill Smith finally speaks, "It is true. I did tell Fred to lie. I know my son jumped in front of the semi-truck on purpose."

Attorney Canton says, "There is an incredibly good chance I can't get your son any money for his accident. The jury might rule your son jumped in front of the truck driver on purpose. If so, they will issue a direct verdict to the truck driver."

"What is a direct verdict Sir?"

"Basically, it means the accident was not your fault."

"What happens now?"

"I go back into the conference room to settle your case."

Bill Smith says, "Sorry we lied. I did it to obtain medical coverage for my son."

Attorney Canton says, "I know the reason you lied. I just wish now we accepted the fifteen million dollars the defense offered us."

Both men say goodbye. Attorney Canton slowly enters the conference room.

Attorney Morgan asks, "Were you able to speak with your client?"

Attorney Canton sits backdown in his chair and replies, "Yes."

"And what did the family say?"

Attorney Canton replies, "I am not telling you. Either we settle or we go to trial."

Attorney Morgan replies, "Do you really want to go to trial with the new evidence we have?"

"If we do not receive a fair settlement, we will go all the way."

Attorney Morgan asks, "What is your final settlement offer?"

"The fifteen million dollars you offered to us recently."

Attorney Morgan shakes his head and says, "No way. I spoke to my insurance client and they are willing to settle for three million dollars. They understand the family will need money for their son's medical condition."

"That is too low," says Attorney Canton. 'I believe a jury would reward us a lot more."

"Or nothing at all," replies Attorney Morgan. "Take the sure money for your client. We strongly believe a jury would see it our way, that your client stepped in front of the semi-truck on purpose. We can show his state of mind with the letter and Fred Harris's confession."

Attorney Canton stands up and says, "See you in court then. Let us continue the depositions in the morning."

Attorney Morgan replies, "I will bring in Robin Smith at ten am."

Attorney Canton says, "I thought Robin was out West."

Attorney Morgan replies, "No, my investigator, Gavin Parker, located her in Tacoma, Washington and escorted her bac to Gulfport."

Attorney Canton says, "Her deposition will be very interesting to take."

"I agree with you."

Attorney Canton exits the conference room.

Attorney Morgan turns to Gavin and says, "Have Robin looking nice and in my office at 9 am sharp."

"No problem, sir." Gavin stands up, shakes his client's hand, and leaves the conference room.

Back in his Honda, Gavin calls Sharon.

"Hello Sharon. I am coming to pick you both up. Robin's deposition is tomorrow at 10 am. My client wants her in his office at 9 am. Your sister needs to rest so she will look pretty in the morning. What is she doing now?"

"My sister and our mother are watching television and drinking beer."

"Have her stop drinking now. I will be there in twenty-five minutes."

Sharon replies, "Will do, see you soon."

Gavin calls Cindy on her cell phone.

"Hi Cindy."

"It is always good to hear your voice, Gavin. What is going on?"

"I am on my way to pick my witness and her sister up in Ocean Springs. Robin's deposition is tomorrow at ten am. I am calling to see if you would like to have lunch with us?"

"I would love too. I am at work today."

"How about us three pick you up and we all walk to Taco Bell. We can also see if the construction crew whistles at me."

Cindy laughs at that comment and replies, "I am free from noon to one pm."

"We will see you in the lobby of your building at noon."

"Deal, thanks for calling me, Gavin."

"My pleasure. I always love hearing your voice."

Cindy laughs and says, "That is nice to know. Bye."

Gavin arrives at Sharon's mother house in Ocean Springs and rings the doorbell.

Sharon opens the door and yells, "The Uber Taxi driver is here."

Gavin laughs and replies, "I will wait for you both in my car."

Sharon replies, "We will be out in five minutes."

A few minutes later Robin and Sharon enters his Honda. Robin sits in the front seat.

Gavin speaks to the ladies on the way to Gulfport.

"We will stop at the hotel in case you want to change clothes, then we will have lunch with a woman I like, then we will discuss Robin's deposition tomorrow."

Robin says, "Sounds like a plan."

Sharon asks, "Tell us about this woman you like, Gavin."

"Her name is Cindy. She woks for the law firm of Morgan and Rodgers as their receptionist. We had lunch the other day and it went well. I think she is twenty-four years old. Cindy is five-feet-two inches and has long blonde hair. I haven't asked her out on an official date yet."

Robin asks, "Why not?"

Gavin replies, "If she says no or has a boyfriend, I have to face her every time I visit the client. It would make me uncomfortable."

Sharon laughs and replies, "Take a chance, move in on her before someone else does."

Robin adds, "I bet all the single lawyers in her office have asked her out."

Sharon says, "I can't wait to meet her today."

Robin says, "I have a plan. Gavin. You pretend you must go to the rest room or pretend you must take a phone call. When we are alone with her, we will find out for you if she has a boyfriend, if she wants to go out with you and what she thinks of you as a person."

"Deal", says Gavin as he pulls up to the building his PI firm is in. "Wait her, I will be only a few minutes. Our next stop is the hotel."

Gavin returns to his office and plays back his messages on his answering machine. One is from Virginia Farmer. Gavin gives the woman a call on her cell phone.

"Hello?"

"Hi, Virginia, this is Gavin Parker of Parker Investigations, how have you been?"

"Hello, Gavin, I was wondering if the law firm of Morgan and Rodgers issued you a case."

"An excessively big one. I am still working it. I had to fly to Tacoma and escort a witness, I found a letter showing that the plaintiff stepped in front of a semi-truck on purpose and…"

"How old was the plaintiff when he or she died?"

"The plaintiff lived and is a paraplegic at the age of twenty-four."

"How sad."

"After my case is finished, I will come over and I will tell you all about it over lunch."

"Ok, sounds like an exciting case. I can't wait to hear about it."

Both Gavin and Virginia say good-bye.

A few minutes later and Gavin returns to his Honda.

"Next stop is our hotel. I will wait in the car for you both to return after changing clothes."

Sharon says, "My sister and I will be quick. We want to meet this, Cindy."

Gavin drives the four miles to the hotel and lets the two women out. The women run into the hotel. Gavin turns his car radio on to a country station.

Thirty minutes go by before the two women emerge from the hotel. Both are wearing blue jeans and tank tops.

As they enter the car Gavin says" Ladies, you will get whistled at from the construction crew we have to walk by to go to lunch."

Sharon laughs and replies, "I sure do hope so."

Gavin drives to the parking lot of Morgan and Rodgers law firm. He turns to the two ladies and says, "I will be right back with Cindy."

Gavin rides the elevator to the 9th floor and enters the law firm. Cindy is sitting at the reception desk with another woman.

Cindy smiles and says, "Gavin, meet Rebecca. I am training her to take my place."

"Hello, Rebecca." Gavin turns his attention to the woman he is crazy about and asks, "Where are you going?"

Cindy says, "I am going to attend law school. I want to be a lawyer really bad."

Gavin laughs and says, "I can see you in court now arguing your case."

"I will be calling on you to do all my investigative work, Gavin," says Cindy.

"That is nice to hear. Are you ready for lunch?"

Cindy stands up, grabs her purse, and says, "I am ready."

Gavin asks Rebecca, "Can I bring you something back from the restaurant?"

Rebecca smiles and replies, "Can you bring me back a small salad?"

Gavin looks at her and asks, "Is that all you want? I am treating."

Rebecca says, "Yes. I am not a big eater."

Gavin and Cindy start to leave the law firm when Rebecca says, "Have a nice lunch."

Cindy says, "Thanks, we will. We will be back in forty-five minutes.

Gavin walks Cindy to his car. He opens both right side doors and the two women step out.

Sharon & Robin introduce themselves and give Cindy a hug.

The four walks down the sidewalk talking. They soon come across the construction crew standing on rafters. The men stop working, but they do not whistle. The foreman is also with his men on the rafters. Gavin spots him and waves. The foreman waves back. Gavin and the women walk on.

Cindy says, "Wow, no whistles. That is a nice change."

Sharon laughs and says, "I wish they did whistle."

The four soon arrive at their destination and they grab a corner booth. The young waitress walks over to take their drink orders.

Gavin says to the waitress, "One check please and I will take it."

The four are having a nice lunch when Gavin says, "Sorry, but I have to call one of my clients." Gavin exits the restaurant and is on his cell phone in the parking lot.

Sharon says to Cindy, I like Gavin a lot. He is a true gentleman."

Cindy says, "I agree with you. I liked him from the moment I laid eyes on him when he visited the law firm almost a week ago today."

Robin asks Cindy, "Are you single, married or what?"

"I had a boyfriend till two months ago, when he texted me goodbye."

Sharon replies, "What? He texted you goodbye."

Yes, he is in the Army, stationed in Germany. We dated for almost a year. I know now, long distance relationships do not work."

"Robin says, "I know Gavin is single. He just works too many hours."

Cindy says, "I wouldn't' mind being his girlfriend. I think he is just too shy to ask me to be his mate."

Sharon says, "I know one thing, you both would make a nice couple."

A few minutes later Gavin returns to the table and asks, "Did I miss anything?"

Cindy replies, "No, we were just talking girl talk."

The group have a nice lunch and walk back to the law firm. The construction crew are not on the job when they walked by.

Robin slips Gavin a note during the walk. 'Gavin, Cindy is single and likes you very much, so ask her for a date.'

The two women wait in the Honda while Gavin rides the elevator with Cindy to the law firm on the nineth floor.

"Cindy, I hope you had a nice lunch."

"I did. We have to do this more often till I have to quit the law firm for college."

Gavin shyly says, "Cindy, I would like us to go out, like boyfriend and girlfriend."

Cindy exits the elevator and stops in front of the law firm door. "I was hoping you would ask me to be your Girlfriend." Cindy then gives Gavin a quick kiss and enters the office.

Gavin walks to his Honda and enters, both women say, "Well, did you ask her to be your girlfriend?"

"I did and Cindy said yes right away. Thanks for passing me the note, Robin."

Sharon replies, "Treat her special. She is a nice woman."

Gavin starts the car, and they exit the parking lot.

Bill Smith contacts his attorney.

"Sir, I am sorry for the deception. I had to do it. We need medical coverage for our son."

Attorney Canton replies, "I know you are sorry for the deception, Bill. Now the problem we face is, either settle for what we can get or go all the way to trial and pray the jury rewards us an amount."

Bill asks, "What are the chances we win our case?"

"I think less than fifty percent. All the new evidence hurts us. The jury everyday viewing your son in his wheelchair, will cause some jurors to hold out for you. So, it is a tossup. The worry I have is we lose in trial and we receive no money for your son. Our best bet is to settle. I will call Attorney Morgan and will feel him out. Talk to you later. Cross your fingers Attorney Morgan has a heart."

Attorney Morgan is sitting with his partner in the lunchroom when Attorney Canton calls him.

"Henry, this is Joe. Do you have a moment?"

"Yes, I am in our office lunchroom with my partner."

"I spoke to Bill Smith and we want to settle. What is your bottom dollar amount?"

"My client feels awful about your client's medical condition. They realize how much care he needs around the clock. They also know if they give you no money the media will eat them up in the newspapers as cold hearted. So, I am authorized to give you three million dollars."

Attorney Canton replies, "We will accept your offer. My client says he is sorry for the deception."

Attorney Morgan says, "I will draw up the settlement papers and have them delivered to you later today."

Attorney Canton replies, "Speak to you soon."

Attorney Morgan takes a bite of his sandwich and says to his partner, "The Smith case is settled for three million dollars. We saved a lot of money and dodged a bullet."

Attorney Rodgers says, "Thank God our private investigator discovered the suicidal letter in the garage."

"You are absolutely right. That letter proved the true state of mind the young man was in about Robin divorcing him. A sad case for sure. I feel for the family," says Attorney Morgan.

Gavin is back in his hotel room resting when his cell phone caller id shows that the law firm of Morgan and Rodgers is calling.

'This is Gavin Parker."

"I am calling to inform you that we do not have to take Robin's deposition. We just settled the case for three million dollars thanks to you discovering the letter."

"Great news, sir. I know Robin will be happy to know about the cancelled deposition."

"Have her come by at ten am tomorrow anyway. I want to meet the woman."

Gavin asks, "Can you return her original letter?

"I will have it in an envelope in your name at the front desk."

Gavin replies, "Thank you, sir. Let me go now. I have to make my airline reservations for Tacoma."

Attorney Morgan says, "Do not forget to give me your timesheet."

"No sir I won't. I will work on it during my flight to Tacoma."

Gavin and Attorney Morgan say their goodbyes. Gavin then knocks on Robin's door.

"Come in she says loudly.

Gavin says, "your deposition has been cancelled. They just settled for three million dollars."

"Is that a good settlement amount?"

"The demand at one time was thirty million dollars."

Robin asks, "can you drive me to Dean's residence. I want to speak to him in person.?"

Gavin replies, "let us go now then. Attorney Morgan wants us to come by around ten am just to meet you. Now when do you ladies want to fly back home?"

Robin says, "I may just stay here and take care of Dean."

Sharon says, "I am ready to fly back to Tacoma now. I miss my boyfriend so much."

Gavin says, "I will wait to see what happens between your sister and Dean before booking the return flight. It may just be you and I flying back."

In the ride over to Dean's house Robin says," I feel so sorry for my actions. If I never filed for divorce Dean would be walking."

Gavin replies, "love works in mysterious ways."

Fifteen minutes later Gavin pulls up in the driveway of Dean's house.

Eva is watering her plants when she sees Robin exiting Gavin's car.

"Ronin", she says putting down the garden hose while running over to greet her.

"Can I see Dean?"

"Of course, he is watching television with Bill in the living room."

Eva and Robin enters the house. Gavin pulls out a notepad and starts working on his time sheet.

An hour goes by before Robin emerges from Dean's residence.

Gavin exits his car. Robin says, "I am staying in Gulfport. Dean and I are getting back together. He is in awfully bad shape. I cried when I first saw him sitting in his wheelchair. Can I call you later to pick me up?"

Gavin nods his head up and down and give Robin a big hug. Robin reenters Dean's residence and Gavin departs the area.

While driving back to the hotel Gavin makes several phone calls.

"Sharron, your sister met with Dean and his family. She is staying in Gulfport. Her and Dean are getting back together."

"My sister was up all night reading her bible. She always loved him."

"I am coming back to the hotel. I will take a long nap, then we will go out to eat. Care for anything special"

Sharon says, "I am dying for a good thick steak."

"Steak it is. I will knock on your door in a few hours."

Gavin contacts Cindy.

"The case settled for three million dollars and Robin is staying in Gulfport. Her and Dean are getting back together."

Cindy replies, "I am glad Robin and Dean are getting back together. I was just about to call you. Attorney Morgan wants you to forget making a time sheet. Just call and give him an amount for your time and expenses for this past week."

Gavin says, "I will. Do you want to join me and Sharon for a steak dinner tonight?"

Cindy laughs and replies, "Just what I wanted, a three-person date. Yes, I want to join you both."

Gavin asks, "What is your home address?"

Cindy gives it to her boyfriend.

"We will pick you up at seven pm. See you then."

Gavin is back in the hotel when Robin calls him.

"Can you please come and pick me up?"

"I will be there in about fifteen minutes."

Gavin tells Sharon where he is going.

"I will be back before dinner."

Gavin listens to a country music station on the way to Dean Smith's residence.

Robin is standing outside when Gavin pulls up in the driveway.

Gavin asks as Robin enters his car, "I am surprised you called so soon."

"Dean had to get his rest. He is in awfully bad shape. He is lucky to be alive. Bill told me the whole story of the accident and why he tried to deceive the insurance company."

Gavin replies, "The family is incredibly lucky the insurance company for the truck line is giving them any money. If they went to trial, I am sure the jury would issue the truckline a direct verdict."

"What is a direct verdict?"

"It is when the jury finds for the insurance defense law firm and they have to pay zero."

Robin says, "I wish I never told Dean the night of the party that I filed for divorce."

Gavin says, "Do you know Dean wears your wedding ring on a chain around his neck?"

"No. When I saw him, he was wrapped around a blanket."

"I guess you will live with your mother."

"No, The Smith family have a third bedroom. Eva is getting the room ready as we speak."

At seven pm, your sister, Cindy and I are having dinner at a steak place. Do you care to join us?"

"No. I am tired. I plan to sleep all night in my bed at the hotel."

Gavin arrives at the hotel and opens Robin's car door.

Robin says, "You are a true gentleman."

Gavin takes a shower and gets ready for his dinner date.

Sharon knocks on Gavin's bedroom door and says softly, "Robin is asleep. I am ready when you are."

On the drive over to Cindy's Gavin asks, "Will it bother you if I listen to a country radio station."

"I hate country, how about a pop station."

Gavin laughs and replies, "I will fulfill your wish."

Sharon says, "I am glad you like Cindy."

"I am crazy for her. I just wish I had a nine to five job like most people have. Then I could spend more time with her."

"Just quit the PI business and do something else," says Sharon.

"I just might do that."

Cindy is standing outside in a pink dress. She waves when Gavin pulls up. Sharon exits the passenger front seat and sits in back. Gavin closes the passenger door once Cindy enters.

Sharon says quickly, "I am glad you are dating Gavin. He is truly a nice man."

Gavin enters the Honda and says, "Too bad Robin didn't want to join us."

Cindy asks, "Why not?"

Sharon says, "My sister was tired. When we got back to the hotel room, she fell asleep with her clothes on."

Gavin says, Robin is staying in Gulfport and will live with the Smith family. She also is getting back together with Dean."

Cindy replies, "Wow, from getting a divorce to moving back in with him, I never saw that coming."

"Neither did I," says Gavin as they pull up to The Farley Stake House.

Gavin, Cindy, and Sharon have a nice dinner over a bottle of wine before they all called it a night.

James Paul Ellison

DAY 8 – TUESDAY

The next morning at eight am, Robin returns to the hotel room wearing a wet bathing suit under her white robe. She says to her sister who is having coffee, "The indoor pool is warm. I was the only person there."

Sharon replies, "I am going to see our mother today. Do you want to come with me?"

"Not today, I want to go visit with Dean and his family."

Sharon replies, Gavin is making our airline reservations to fly back to Tacoma. We plan to fly back maybe late tomorrow or the following morning."

Robin says, "Now that I am staying in Gulfport, I can visit with mom anytime."

"Just don't get drunk with her," Sharon says.

Robin laughs and says, "If we go to any bar, I will drink coke only."

There is a knock on their interior door.

"Come in Gavin, we are dressed."

Gavin enters dressed in blue jeans and a dark blue polo shirt. He says to Sharon, "We fly out tomorrow evening at seven pm on Delta. We have one stop over in Dallas, then home to Tacoma to your boyfriend."

Sharon smiles and replies, "Great, I will have by boyfriend pick us up."

"Tell him it is flight # 3232."

"Flight 3232, got it," says Sharon.

"Let us go downstairs and have the hotel breakfast. We have to be at Attorney Morgan's office at ten am."

Robin says, "You two go first. I still must shower and change. I will eat something later."

Sharon and Gavin start to leave the hotel room when Sharon says, "We will bring you something to eat when we get back."

Sharon and Gavin exit the hotel room. Robin hops in the shower.

Twenty minutes later, Robin is fully dressed. She sits on her bed and calls Dean's house. Eva answers.

"Morning Robin, your room is already."

"I plan to come over there after I speak with the attorney that was against you."

Eva asks, "Why were you listed as a witness against us?"

"Because they told me they wanted to know about the party and what conversations Dean, and I had that night. How is Dean doing this morning.?"

"He had a bad night; he was up almost the entire night. He did not mention your name. Dean has memory loss."

"Will Dean's memory come back?"

"His doctors say it will with time."

The two women talk till Sharon and Gavin return from breakfast. Sharon is caring a small plate covered with foil.

"Here you go sis, I brought you sausage and eggs."

Robin says goodbye to Eva. She turns to her sister and says, "Thank you. I am hungry now."

Thirty minutes later Gavin knocks and enters their room. "We have to go now to the law firm." All three leave. Robin sits up front and says while putting her seatbelt on, "I am glad there is no deposition to take."

Gavin replies as he departs the hotel's parking lot, "No, we are going to have a friendly talk only with the attorneys. I will be with you in the conference room."

Gavin, Robin, and Sharon walk into the law office of Morgan & Rodgers. They walk up to Cindy who greets them with a smile. Cindy introduces the group to her replacement. "Let me introduce you all to, Rebecca."

The group greet her with hellos and Gavin says, "I am a private investigator that your firm uses. You will be seeing me often, I hope. The two ladies are visiting from Tacoma, Washington. We are here to meet with Attorney Morgan."

Cindy looks at Rebecca and says, "Go ahead and greet the group, then seat them in the lobby. Contact Barbara, Attorney Morgan's secretary, extension 44, and advise her Gavin is here for his ten am meeting."

Rebecca smiles and says to the group, "Good morning, welcome to the law firm of Morgan and Rodgers. How can we help you?"

Gavin helps the new receptionist role play. "I have a ten am appointment with Attorney Morgan. My name is Gavin Parker of Parker Investigations."

"Please have a seat in the lobby. I will let the attorney know you are here."

Cindy says to Rebecca, "That was easy, right?

Rebecca nods and asks, "Can I go to the restroom?

Cindy replies, "Sure."

After Rebecca walks away, Gavin asks Cindy, "How is she doing on the job?"

Cindy looks around and in a low voice says, "Today is here last day. She gets too nervous talking to people and forgets what she has to do."

Gavin replies, "Have the firm hire Robin. She needs a job now that she will stay in Gulfport, instead of going back to Tacoma."

Robin speaks up, "I would love to work here, and I am not afraid to speak up when I need to."

Cindy laughs and says, "I can see that. I will speak to Barbara about it and have her speak with you after your meeting with the attorney."

Robin says, "Thanks," just as Rebecca returns from the rest room.

The group sits in the waiting room for a few minutes before Barbara walks over.

"Hello Gavin. Which one of you two ladies is Robin?"

Robin stands up and says, "I am Robin."

Barbara shakes her hand and says, "It is nice to meet you. Please follow me to Attorney Morgan's office."

Gavin says, "This is Sharon, Robin's older sister. Can we come to?"

Barbara replies, "Why not, it is a meeting after all."

Barbara escorts all three to her boss's office. He stands up when the group walks in.

Barbara says, "You already know Gavin." Barbara points as she speaks. "This is Robin and her sister Sharon."

Attorney Morgan shakes all their hands and points to some chairs. "Please have a seat."

Barbara asks, "Can I get any of you a drink?"

Robin speaks up. "I would like a coke."

"We do, I will be right back with your coke."

Attorney Morgan looks at Robin and Sharon and says, "We brought you both all the way from Tacoma. I have never been to that city."

Sharon says, "I have lived there almost my entire life."

Robin says, "It is too cold for me and there is hardly any sun. I am staying in Gulfport and will take care of Dean Smith."

The group have a friendly meeting that last forty minutes. As they start to leave the office, Attorney Morgan asks Gavin to stay behind.

The two ladies return to the waiting room. Robin asks Cindy, "Where is Rebecca?"

"She is at lunch from 11 am to noon. Let me see if Barbara has a free minute."

Cindy picks up the telephone and dials an extension. She then asks, "Barbara, can you come to the reception desk please?"

A few minutes later Barbara walks out to the reception desk.

Cindy says, "As you know Rebecca is not working out as our new receptionist. Robin just moved back to Gulfport from Tacoma, Washington and is looking for a job. Can I train her to be our new receptionist?"

Barbara replies as she looks at Robin, "Let me interview her. Robin, please come to my office."

As the two women walk off, Sharon gives the thumbs up to Cindy.

Attorney Morgan says to Gavin sitting across from him, "You did an excellent job for the firm. How would you like to be our inhouse investigator?"

Gavin asks, "What would my job duties entail and what kind of pay am I looking at a week?"

"We would start at seven hundred dollars a week. The work hours are from nine am to five pm, Monday to Friday with weekends off."

"It would be nice to have a steady job. In the PI business you are waiting for the telephone to ring. Does medical coverage come with the job?"

Attorney Morgan says, "You will have full medical coverage and two weeks' vacation. We also have a 401 retirement plan you can join."

What would my job duties be?"

"You will have your own office, all fifteen lawyers would be dropping off assignments for you to work on, from running data to investigating cases like you just did for me on the Dean Smith case."

Gavin reaches over and shakes his new boss's hand. "I would love to work for you and this firm."

Attorney Morgan says, "I was hoping you would join us. You did an excellent job on mine. By the way, how much do we owe you for this case?"

Gain says, "I do not know yet. I had to fly to Tacoma, Washington to pick up the witness and I am escorting her sister back to Tacoma tonight, plus being with them day and night for five days and ......"

Attorney Morgan interrupt's Gavin and says, "How about we pay you a flat fee of twenty-five thousand dollars. Fifteen thousand for the Dean Smith case and a ten-thousand-dollar bonus for joining the firm."

Gavin cannot believe what he is hearing and says, "Sir, that is more than enough for sure."

"Well, Gavin, I want you happy and I want you to be with this firm for a long time."

Gavin laughs and replies, "Oh, I plan to retire with your firm."

"Good to hear. Let me get my secretary to write me a check."

Attorney Morgan picks up his telephone and dials an extension.

"Barbara can you please come to my office now and bring the firm's checkbook with you."

"Yes sir."

Barbara enters a few minutes later with the checkbook.

Attorney Morgan says to her, "Please join us. Write a check for twenty-five thousand dollars made out to Gavin Parker. On the memo section write ten thousand for The Drew Smith case, slash fifteen thousand bonus." I want you to be the first to know, the firm just hired Gavin to be our inhouse investigator. Find him an office and escort him there after we are finished here. Oh, and introduce him to all the firm's staff."

Barbara looks over at Gavin and says, "It is great you are joining the firm. I look forward to working with you, Gavin."

Gavin replies, "It will be fun working with you too. What about business cards for me?"

Attorney Morgan says, "Make your own and put the cost on your expense sheet. Let me look over the draft of your business cards before they are printed. Have the firm name, address and telephone on the cards, plus your name and title as private investigator."

"Will do, sir."

Barbara hands the check over for her boss to sign.

Attorney Morgan signs the check and hands it over to Gavin, "Here you go young man."

Gavin takes the check and says, "I will start on Monday when I return from escorting Sharon to Tacoma."

Barbara says, "Let us find you an office and introduce you to the employees of the firm."

As Barbara and him are leaving attorney Morgan's large corner office Gavin asks, "Can I have an office with a window?"

Barbara laughs and says, "Why do you ask that question?"

Gavin replies, "I just didn't want my office to be the old broom closet."

Fifteen minutes later Gavin is back in the lobby. Sharon is still waiting for her sister to return.

Gavin goes over to Cindy and whispers, "You are looking at the firms new inhouse investigator."

Cindy says, "Really?"

Gavin nods his head up and down and returns to his seat in the waiting room.

A woman brings Robin to the waiting room and says goodbye.

Robin says to her group, "That is Dawn, she is the personnel director. I am hired and I start on Monday at fifteen an hour."

Robin walks over and whispers the same thing to Cindy.

Gavin says, "We can all leave now."

Cindy gives Robin a thumb's up as they leave the law office.

In the elevator Gavin shows the women his check.

Both women say, "Wow."

Sharon adds, "I know who is treating us to lunch."

Gavin says, "You two are looking at the inhouse private investigator of the law firm of Morgan and Rodgers."

Robin asks, "What about your own pi firm, Parker Investigations?"

Gavin laughs and says, "I was starving as I tried to grow my start-up pi firm. I had only one client. A woman named Virginia Farmer. She just retired from the insurance business. I sat in my office playing video games and waiting for my phone to ring. Now I have a good job, steady hours, and a paycheck. You can't beat that."

Sharon says, "We need to check out of the hotel."

Gavin replies, "That is my next stop."

Robin asks, "After we check out can you drop me off at my mother's?"

"No problem," says Gavin.

The group soon arrives at the Hilton Hotel. They quickly pack-up and go to the front desk. Gavin pays the hotel invoice with his credit card and they exit the building.

Once in the Honda Robin says, "I sure did like the indoor swimming pool."

"Where do you ladies want to eat at?

Robin says, "I am not hungry yet. I will eat something at Dean's."

Sharon says, "Let us stop at Taco Bell and get soft tacos to go."

Robin speaks up and says, "Thanks Gavin for helping me land the reception job at your place of employment."

"I know you will be an excellent receptionist."

Gavin soon arrives at Dean Smith's residence. Robin collects her belongings and gives her sister a big hug. "See you around sis."

Sharon watches her sister walk away and enter the residence. She turns to Gavin and says, "Take me over to my mother so I can say goodbye, please."

"No problem."

Twenty or so minutes later Gavin pulls up in front of the bar. Sharon says, "I won't be long. One beer with my mom and then we can go to Taco Bell."

Gavin plays a country radio station as he waits for Sharon.

Sharon soon comes out crying. "Saying goodbye is always hard."

Gavin drives away from the bar and replies, I agree."

They make one stop to Gavin's bank before arriving at a Taco Bell drive-up window. They sit in the parking lot to have their meals.

Sharon says, "I thank you for this lunch and for everything you have done for me and my sister since we met."

"No problem. This journey we have been on has been great," says Gavin.

Sharon says, "I have a change of plans. I will fly out alone tonight. My boyfriend will be waiting for me at the Tacoma Airport to take me home."

"You are sure, Sharon?"

"I am sure. It is a long flight to Tacoma and back to Gulfport just to escort me home."

Gavin asks, "What do we do till your flight, we have like five hours."

Sharon says, "Let us kill time at a cinema. I haven't seen a movie in at least a year."

Gavin replies, "There is a sixteen-screen cinema complex only a few miles from here."

Gavin and Sharon soon arrive at the cinema. They select a movie and enter the building. Gavin buys a large box of popcorn and two cokes. They then enter the almost empty theater and sit up high. They recline back and wait for the room to go dark.

Gavin says, "I may fall asleep. I have been going non-stop for days."

"Go ahead, I won't wake you."

The theater goes dark and the movie commercials then start to play.

Sharon says, "This is the part I don't like. I am forced to watch stupid commercials and future showings."

Gavin laughs and says, "I know how you feel."

When the movie is over and the lights come back on, Sharon must wake Gavin.

"Wake up, Gavin. It is time to leave."

"How long did I sleep?"

"Since the fourth commercial. The good thing is you don't snore."

Gavin laughs and replies, "Let me take you to the airport now."

The Gulfport International Airport is terribly busy.

Sharon asks Gavin, "Why is this place busy?"

"Gulfport has twelve casinos and the casinos run junkets."

"What is a junket.?"

"That is where they offer customers a free hotel stay and give them free play money to start gambling. The casino hopes you will spend all your time in their establishment and loose all your money playing their many slots."

"Lucky for me I am not a gambler. I love staying home with a hot cup of coffee and a good book," says Sharon as she yawns.

Gavin sees Sharon yawning and replies, "Guess you will be sleeping on the plane ride to Tacoma."

Gavin drops Sharon off in front of the terminal and says, "I will be right behind as soon as I park my car."

A porter walks over to Sharon and asks, "Can I carry your luggage for you, Miss?"

"Yes please, to the Delta airline counter."

Gavin soon arrives and sits with Sharon at her gate.

Sharon says, "In Tacoma they do not let you sit at the gate unless you are flying out."

"Gulfport relies on happy casino customers returning to their city, so they allow us to wait with you at the gate."

The airline employee announces the flight to Seattle with a stopover in Dallas.

"That is my flight", says Sharon. She gives a big hug to Gavin and says, "Please take care of my baby sister for me."

"I will. Have a nice nap home," says Gavin.

Both hug one more time before Sharon walks thru the doorway to her flight. Gavin stays to watch the plane go air born.

Gavin is almost home to his apartment when his cell phone rings. Caller ID shows it to be the law firm of Morgan and Rodgers.

"This is private investigator Gavin Parker."

"Afternoon Gavin, this is Attorney Rodgers. Please come by my office when you return from Tacoma. I have a new assignment I need your help on."

Gavin replies, "I am free now. Sharon wanted to fly home alone."

"Good, come see me now then."

Gavin asks, "Is this case about another semi-truck accident?"

"No. Sadly it is about a teenager that died playing on a steam roller machine at a closed mall last night. He was waiting for his father to pick him up and found a steam roller machine behind the mall, started it up, played on it and jumped off. His pants leg got caught in the machine and the machine rolled over him. He was only fifteen."

Gavin asks, "Who do you represent, sir?"

"I represent Sunshine Mall."

Gavin says, I will see you in about twenty-five minutes."

Gavin turns his radio on to a country station and sings along to a tune.

THE END